A Brother's Justice

William Cutler

A Brother's Justice

Text copyright © 2013 William Cutler
First printed edition © 2023 William Cutler

All rights reserved. No part of this book my be reproduced,
distributed, or transmitted in any form or by any means including
photocopying, recording, or other electronic methods, without
written permission of the publisher, except in the case of brief
quotations embodied in critical reviews and certain other
noncommercial uses permitted by copyright law.

To request permission, contact the publisher at
publishing@villagebooks.com

This is a work of fiction. Names, characters, places,
and incidents either are the products of the author's imagination
or are used fictitiously. Any resemblance to actual persons,
living or dead, is entirely coincidental.

ISBN 979-8-218-20561-4

Library of Congress Control Number: 2023908967

Designed by Jill Flores

Printed by Village Books
1200 11th Street
Bellingham, WA 98225

To a very patient wife, my girls,
and Dave and Jeremy.
In memory of David

Special thanks to:
Chris Flieger and Miguel Hernandez
for their technical support

PROLOGUE

Sunday nights were usually quiet, especially just before shift change. Officer Bill Cunningham sat in his patrol car in an alley just off of Northwest Sixth Street. He worked the evening shift and patrolled the northwest section of Fort Lauderdale known as District II. Bill patiently waited for the midnight shift to begin advising over the radio that they were on duty so he could go home. This area of town is home to lower income families and the crime rate in the district reflected its makeup, which is why Cunningham liked to work District Two; he was usually never bored, but this was a particularly slow Sunday night.

"Charlie 42."

Cunningham looked at his watch: 10:45 p.m. He wondered why the dispatcher would be trying to give him a call when he only had fifteen minutes left on his shift. Bill was tired and wanted to go home. He reluctantly pushed the talk button on his radio to respond.

"Charlie 42, you've got to be kidding."

"Wish I was. I need you to respond to the Hill Hotel. Reports of a woman screaming in the alley."

"Charlie 42, in route." The tone of his voice revealed his displeasure at getting the late call. Cunningham put his unit in drive and pulled out onto Sixth Street. The Hill Hotel was just one block over and not really a hotel at all. That was the nickname the cops in the district gave to a rundown apartment complex owned by Willie Hill. The "hotel" was home to hookers, pimps and drug dealers, so reports of screaming coming from the Hill Hotel were not that unusual.

Cunningham pulled his patrol car into the alley at the rear of the building. Standing in the doorway of apartment number six was Little

Bit, one of the areas resident hookers. Cunningham knew her well. He could not even remember how many times he had arrested her. She was only four feet six inches tall so it was not hard to tell, even in the dark that it was her. No one really knew whether her street name came from her stature or from what she charged for her services, but she was one of the more popular hookers in his zone. The hookers who worked this section of town were not Las Vegas call girls. Five dollars or a rock of cocaine would buy a blow job and whatever disease came along with it.

Bill put his car into park and opened his car door just as Little Bit started towards him. She began to wave frantically as he stepped out of his car to get his attention. A second later, the sound of a gunshot caused Cunningham to dive for cover by the front of his car. As he did, he saw Little Bit falling forward and the figure of a man standing in the doorway directly behind her. He knew in an instant that she had been shot. Cunningham immediately un-holstered his gun and started to assess the situation. He realized that the shot had come from inside the apartment, so he wanted to find out where the man in the doorway had gone. He looked up over the car's hood with his handgun extended out in front of him to survey the scene. Cunningham knew that he needed help, so he keyed the microphone to let the dispatcher know what was happening.

"Charlie 42! Shots fired. Hill Hotel. Rear alley." His voice on the radio was clear and remarkably calm considering what he had just witnessed. He was an experienced officer and even though his heart was pounding wildly, he knew that he needed to be understood if he wanted help to respond. His attention remained fixed on the doorway, so he didn't hear the other units who were now running with their lights and sirens on as they came to his aid. His instincts told him that there was nothing he could do for Little Bit; she was dead, but he needed to get the shooter.

The man in the doorway had apparently not seen the police unit pull up as he pulled the trigger. Cunningham saw the look of shock on the man's face as he stepped out of the apartment to look at Little Bit and realized that he wasn't alone. A split second later, the man was running down the alley with Cunningham in foot pursuit to cut off his escape. The man turned as he ran and began to raise his gun towards Cunningham, but it was too late. Cunningham was too close and dove at the suspect, knocking him to the ground. Before the man knew it, he was laying face down with handcuffs on. Cunningham threw the gun away from the man's side and rolled his suspect over to see who it was.

The first backup units were turning into the alley and Cunningham once again keyed his radio mike. This time it was to let everyone know that the suspect was in custody. He stood up as the first backup officer was running up to him. As he did, he looked back down at the man and immediately recognized him; Johnny Thompson, Little Bit's pimp.

Johnny began yelling something about being innocent, but Cunningham wasn't listening. He left his backup to search Johnny as he walked back to see Little Bit. She was laying face down in a large pool of her own blood. The large entry wound in the center of her back made it clear that there would be no attempts to resuscitate. She was most likely dead before she hit the ground.

As Cunningham looked down at the lifeless body he keyed his mike, "Charlie 42, you can cancel EMS. I'm going to need homicide out here."

Bill switched his radio over to the channel the detective's monitored. He explained to the responding detective of what had just happened in a voice which did not reflect the excitement he'd just been through. A casual listener would have just assumed from his tone that he was reporting on some mundane call rather than having just seen someone killed. Cunningham had worked in this type of environment for a long time and this call was, unfortunately routine to him.

For his quick actions and calmness under fire, Cunningham was transferred to the police department's tactical unit.

Chapter 1

South Florida can be hot any time of year, but it was October and the morning air already felt like midsummer. The sun had begun to creep above the horizon as Bill Cunningham lay motionless in a pool of his own sweat. His clothing had soaked through even though he made sure he positioned himself where there was some protection provided from the shade trees and ornamental plants which lined the office building parking lot he had so carefully picked for his task. Everything was already in motion, so it was too late to make any changes; no matter how uncomfortable he felt.

Well before sunrise, Cunningham had pulled a 1998 Chevrolet van into the South Pointe Medical Center's parking lot. He chose this particular model because it looked identical to the ones used by the landscaping crew who maintained the property and he did not want to attract any undo curiosity as to why it was there. The medical building was four stories tall and typical of the ones which lined South Pine Island Road in Plantation, a bedroom suburb of Ft. Lauderdale. Pine Island Road is a main artery through the city and would be filled with commuter traffic just after the plan was carried out. Proper planning and precise execution would be critical to Bill's success. The parking lot would also soon be full of vehicles from the medical personnel that filled most of the building's offices, but Bill was going to be long gone before they arrived. All he had to do now was wait and let everything unfold as he had planned it.

Cunningham grew up in South Florida and had worked in the Middle East so he knew how to properly dress for this type of weather, but that did not stop him from sweating. Bill moved slightly to see if he could get some relief from the clothes which were now stuck to his body. He was not overly concerned about anyone seeing him at this time of the morning, because the building did not have a security guard on duty. He did not dare move too much though, because there was still a small chance that he could be detected by a passing motorist. He was however, worried about the cameras covering the parking lot and the fact that this building would be the first place investigators would look for evidence. He stayed motionless in his chosen position and mentally reviewed his plan again.

There had been six months of planning leading up to this one day even though the idea had been there for ten years. Bill had come up with the idea shortly after he and his brother, Dave were swindled out of a business which could have made them both millionaires. The swindler's name was Vince Maganelli. What made it worse was that Bill and his brother had been close friends with Vince ever since high school. Bill had dreamt of making Vince pay for his actions, but he had always been too conventional and law abiding to take the law into his own hands. What cemented the idea of getting revenge on Vince was the death of Dave. Their business would have supplied him with the insurance to cover the medical bills from the cancer which was discovered shortly after they were forced out. Dave had waited to go to the doctor until it was too late. They had not made a lot of money from the new business before they left and Dave did not have the extra money to take care of his family and himself at the same time. Bill had made the decision at Dave's funeral that Vince was not going to go unpunished for his greed.

Bill Cunningham had left the Ft. Lauderdale Police Department after sixteen years of service to start up a business with Dave and Vince. He had worked in most of the Department's divisions and knew from his experience how the police would investigate Vince's death. Covering his tracks and making sure investigators would not be charging him for Vince's murder would be the easy part of the plan. There were however, things which needed to be learned to make this an unsolvable crime. He was an experienced investigator and knew what knowledge he needed to obtain to avoid detection and set out to gain these skills. He was also smart enough and meticulous enough to come up with the perfect plan.

Bill had committed to memory every inch of the intersection at South Pine Island Road Drive and Gatehouse Road. He spent hours studying the lay of the land, the traffic patterns and when Vince would appear. It was early morning which meant no wind to disrupt his shot. Cunningham had carefully measured the distance from where he would be positioned to where Vince would stop his car and knew it was exactly two hundred and ten feet away. There were several sites he could have chosen, but this one was the best. He was on a small hill which had enough foliage to allow him to go undetected while he waited. There were also no obstacles between him and the intersection. Traffic would be at a bare minimum and there would not be any pedestrian traffic at this time of the morning, which eliminated the possibility of hurting innocent bystanders. He had even made sure of what days the landscape crew would be there.

He didn't need to, but he ran through the plan just one more time seeing that there was still an hour to go before Vince would be on his mark. He began to check out the sky to see if the weather report was going to be correct when his attention was drawn to a noise he knew he should not be hearing. A white Chevy van had turned off the roadway and was now driving up towards the office building. He recognized it immediately as the lawn maintenance crew. "What the hell are they doing here," Bill muttered to himself as he slightly readjusted his position.

One of the skills Bill had learned in order to carry out his plan was how to make a ghillie suit. A type of camouflage clothing used by snipers that is designed to resemble foliage and covers the wearer from head to toe. Typically, it is a net or cloth garment covered in loose strips of cloth or twine, sometimes made to look like leaves and twigs, and optionally augmented with scraps of foliage from the area. Bill had taken numerous pictures of the plants which lined the hill top he was on and duplicated these plants on his suit. He double checked his suit to make sure it was doing its job of concealing him before turning slowly to see where the van was headed.

"*Holy shit,*" was the only thing Bill could say to himself as he saw the van turn into his section of the parking lot. Even worse, the van pulled into the spot next to his van which was directly behind his hiding place. Bill froze in place. He heard two doors open, then close and then several men speaking in Spanish. Having grown up in South Florida it was almost impossible not to have learned some Spanish, but Bill could not hear them clearly enough to understand what they were saying. Cunningham however, did gather from their tones that they were not happy to be there. He then heard the rear doors of the van open, followed by the sound of a weed eater being started. Bill slowly pulled back the barrel of his rifle which was protruding ever so slightly from out of the ghillie suit. He had been careful to camouflage the rifle in the same way he had done his suit, but didn't want to take any chances. All he could do now was remain perfectly still and see what developed. If he was discovered, it would be a little hard to explain his current attire to the police and he would not get a second chance to get Vince.

Bill's mind began to race as his heart rate climbed. Had he screwed something up in his plan? No, he thought to himself. He had made sure of every detail including when the lawn crew should have been there, so why are they unloading their equipment from the van. Bill fought the adrenalin pumping through his system and said to himself, *Stop. Calm down and think. What's happening here?* Bill quickly came to the conclusion that the lawn service had changed its schedule due to all the rain which had fallen over the past several days. Rain in South Florida is normal and everyone who lives there works around it, so he had not considered the possibility of the lawn crew changing their schedule in his planning, but he had a more immediate problem. He could hear the sound of a gasoline weed eater coming close to his position.

The sound came from his right, but he dare not move to see where the operator was. He could now feel the twigs and small rocks thrown up by the weed eater bouncing off his side as the sound got even closer. Bill had chosen this spot not only for its raised position, but because there were enough plants covering the hill to allow him to blend in. He had positioned himself in a patch of Palmetto Palms and Miscanthus Huron Sunrise which was a tall ornamental grass used in the landscaping around the building's parking lot. Identifying native foliage was yet another thing he had become an expert on since beginning this project. He could now see the head of the weed eater as it spun around just a couple of feet in front of his face. He then saw the legs of its operator who seemed to be moving to the beat of some unheard music. Bill could feel and hear his heart pounding in his chest and hoped that it wasn't loud enough to give away his position.

Cunningham found himself studying the pair of blue jeans and work shoes which were now just a few feet from his face. He was intently watching the scene which was unfolding in front of him for any sign that he had been discovered. He noted that the person, who was now just two or three feet in front of him was short and from the looks of his shoes had spent many hours doing just what he was doing now. He also gave some thought as to what he would do if discovered. Jumping up in front of some man with a weed wacker, while wearing a Ghillie suit and carrying a rifle was not going to go unnoticed. How was he going to make his escape without running the risk of being stopped in his suit? He had heard some wild explanations for unusual situations while he was a cop, but he could not come up with anything that would cover this one. Bill had to admit to himself that this was not a scenario he had even remotely thought of and began to wonder what else he could have missed.

Bill's muscles tightened as he laid there waiting to be discovered. He was still trying to devise an escape plan when he noticed that there was no change in the pace at which the pair of shoes continued along the flower bed. It took what seemed to be an extraordinary amount of time for those shoes to move beyond his line of sight, but finally the sound of the machine indicated that the shoe's owner had passed by without discovering his hiding spot. Bill was in the process of congratulating himself on his ability to construct a ghillie suit when he realized that he had been holding his breath the entire time. He let out a long slow sigh and mentally got his heart and mind back under control. Cunningham listened for any other noises which had the potential to disrupt his plan, but after a few minutes, he heard the crew loading up for what he hoped to be their exit from the parking lot. It took a couple of minutes, but finally the van left the parking lot and headed for the street. Going undiscovered gave Bill renewed confidence that he had indeed come up with a good plan and had done enough research to make the plan work. Now, hopefully all he had to do was lie there and wait.

Bill's attention was once again drawn to how uncomfortable he was and how much he was sweating in the early morning heat. He was more at ease now and allowed himself to move slightly to gain access to some water he was carrying. If someone three feet away didn't discover his hiding spot, he was certain that a camera mounted on a building two hundred feet away wouldn't pick him up either. He drank the water and looked at his watch; 6:45 a.m. A sliver of the sun could be seen just above the horizon now and he knew the phone call would be placed precisely at 6:50 a.m. putting the final phase of the plan into motion.

Now more than ever, Bill had confidence in his plan and that he would not be discovered before he could take his shot. Even if people began showing up for work early they would be parking on the opposite side of the building where the employees were required to park. He was also confident that the silencer he had installed on his rifle would help eliminate the possibility of a passerby being able to identify where the shot came from. Every detail had been covered including where he had positioned his vehicle so he could get back to it and make his escape without being seen. There was a portion of the plan which was out of his control, but the others who he had picked to help him had been thoroughly briefed and would not let him down, because they also had a reason to see the plan succeed. Bill tried to clear his mind. He now had to concentrate on the intersection in front of him and wait for Vince's Mercedes to show up.

A glance at his watch showed that it was now 6:53 a.m. It would take Vince three to four minutes to make it to the intersection once he left his house. It was a demand light, so he would have to stop over the sensors which were buried in the roadway before the traffic light would change from red to green. The vehicle would be stopped for thirty seconds before the light would change, giving Bill more than enough time to make a proper shot. Bill knew that there was one other similar Mercedes SL 550 Roadster in the neighborhood which could be using this intersection and he didn't want to make a mistake. The scope which was mounted to the rifle would make it easy to properly identify the right driver. The minutes clicked by as he began concentrating on his breathing and watching the intersection through his rifle scope. It wasn't long before Bill spotted a Mercedes. He was somewhat startled by the rush of adrenaline which he experienced once he saw the car. He had guessed that he would feel some type of reaction, but had not expected it to be that great. Bill then began to mentally calm himself for what was about to happen.

Cunningham quietly began talking to himself. "OK, take a deep breath. You've made this shot a hundred times so breathe in…exhale, let it out slowly." He slowly and deliberately operated the rifle's bolt to chamber a round. This was his one shot and he didn't want a weapon's malfunction to ruin the plan; not at this point. He was now very controlled in his breathing; practicing the proper technique he had taught himself. He mentally talked himself through the procedure to develop a natural rhythm; *"Breathe in, exhale and hold it. Wait for the natural pause."* Bill had trained with snipers and was taught that this respiratory pause should not be forced or too long. He also knew that if he held his breath for too long it would result in an involuntary movement of his body and throw the bullet off target. A two hundred foot shot is not far by sniper standards, but improper breathing would cause a missed shot. Cunningham had studied long and hard. The text books all said that ten seconds was the time limit he could hold his breath during the natural pause between breaths. This would give him two attempts to get his breathing right before the car would move.

Cunningham carefully reached up with his index finger and pushed the rifle's safety switch to the firing position while maintaining his breathing. For the first time he focused on his target: Vince's head. He had wondered all through the planning stage how he would feel at this very moment and if he would be able to take the shot. It had kept him up some nights worrying if he would actually be able to kill someone in cold blood; even someone he hated as much as Vince. He had taken a human life on several occasions, but those shootings were all in the line of duty and in situations which were very much different than today. Those shootings were always a case of "him or me" situations where someone with a gun was confronted and he had to shoot. Those were all split second decisions where his training had taken over and he did not have time to think of the aftermath of his actions. This was totally different. Right from the start, the plan was always to stop Vince.

None of those thoughts were present now. He was concentrating totally on the task at hand and mentally making sure he was doing everything he had trained himself to do. Shooters call it being "in the bubble" and Cunningham was. As he looked at Vince through the scope he said to himself, *I don't believe it, the asshole is on the phone* as if he shouldn't have been in the last seconds of his life. Bill watched as Vince's eyes moved from looking at the traffic light to looking straight ahead as if he had spotted Bill on the hill in front of him. He exhaled and hit the natural pause between breaths as Vince continued to stare at something in front of him.

Bill began to pull back on the trigger and felt the resistance increase. He continued to pull back until he heard the sound which he had heard so many times before while practicing for today. Because the rifle had been fitted with a silencer, Bill did not hear the sharp crack of a rifle bullet leaving the barrel, but a more subtle sound. One that was more like someone had slapped the surface of a lake with a paddle. At the same instance he heard the sound; he felt the weapon recoil back into his shoulder. A second later he looked out over the top of his scope and watched as the Mercedes rocketed across the intersection and crashed into a light pole on the opposite side of the street.

Cunningham was startled by what he had just seen. He had assumed that the car would remain stopped or worst case, simply coasted out into the intersection. Bill however, did not have the extra time to analyze the situation. There was a car approaching the intersection and he needed to get out of there. Bill carefully slid backwards until he reached the rear door of his van. Taking a quick look around to make sure he was alone, he opened the rear doors and entered the van. It took him only a minute or two to strip off the ghillie suit and jump into the driver's seat.

Bill took just a moment to take a couple of quick breaths to calm himself down. He still needed to remain calm. There were now a couple of cars stopped out on the roadway and several people were standing around Vince's car. They would certainly take notice of a van rushing away from the scene. Bill calmly put the van into drive and pulled out of the parking lot.

Cunningham was not concerned about anyone jotting down information pertaining to a van leaving the scene of what appeared to be an accident. He had made sure that the van could not be traced back to him. Bill had not purchased the van. It was nondescript, the windows were tinted and the license could not be traced. He had visited several junk yards before he was able to grab a license plate from a similar make and model van. Running the tags to find the owner of the van would be a dead end for the police. Bill pulled out onto Pine Island Road and took a quick look at Vince's car in his rear view mirror as he drove away. Bystanders blocked his view of Vince, but he was sure he had accomplished what he had set out to do.

CHAPTER 2
(THIRTY TWO YEARS EARLIER)

Football practice had been cut short due to an afternoon thunderstorm and Bill Cunningham wanted to get home to study for a chemistry test he had the next day. He and his brother had just driven out of the Plantation High school parking lot when Dave spotted someone he knew walking on the side of the road. He looked over at Bill who was driving and said "Hey, that's the new guy in my class. Pull over and give him a ride." Bill wanted to keep on going, not only because he was totally unprepared for the test and needed the extra time to study, but because the guy was soaked and he didn't want to ruin the seats of his new car. Dave, even more demanding said "pull over" and before Bill could even get the car stopped the passenger door was open and Dave was yelling for the guy to hurry up and get in.

Bill looked at the kid who was now dripping all over his car's freshly cleaned interior. He was their age, about 16 with jet black hair that was combed back and hung over his collar. He was about average height and generally had kind of a chunky appearance. Bill wasn't overly impressed.

"Hey man, thanks for the lift. I thought I was going to drown out there. Is it always this way?" Bill looked into the rear view mirror at the guy who was now dripping on his seats.

"Only from April to October. You must be new to the area."

"Yeah, we just moved in over the summer from New York."

Before Bill could respond with his opinion of New Yorkers, Dave piped in and said "You're in my English class. What's your name?"

"Vince, Vince Maganelli."

Bill followed Vince's directions and dropped him off at his home.

The three became good friends in the months that followed and Vince easily assimilated himself into the small group of friends the brothers had grown up with. With the exception of Vince, the group had all known each other since elementary school and was very tight. It was the mid 70's and even though Ft. Lauderdale was a vacation area there was not a lot to do if you were in high school. The group usually found themselves hanging out at the beach on the weekends, participating in school sports or going to the movies. They all came from what would be considered middle class families, so they all had cars and "cruise'n" the beach on a Saturday night was almost mandatory.

Bill Cunningham had just got a 1970 Dodge Charger R/T for his sixteenth birthday and since it was bigger than the other guys' cars, he usually drove when they headed out on Saturday nights. Dave only had a restricted license, but Jay Goldman, who referred to himself as the group's "token Jew" had a 1971 Pontiac Firebird which he waxed almost every Saturday morning before doing anything else. Nicky Schapone, not to be outdone called himself the group's "token Italian." He had a Vega, which was new and he had worked on its performance. Ken Martin was the quiet one of the group and drove his parent's Chevrolet Monte Carlo. No one suspected that it had a 454 cubic inch motor under the hood and would "kick some ass" in a drag race. Ken did not spend a dime of his own money to buy gas his entire time in high school. He won his money by beating unsuspecting racers at the Saturday night drag races out on Flamingo Road with the family car.

Then Vince entered the picture. He had a 1968 Volkswagen "Bug" which was bright yellow in color. The vehicle had issues. Vince carried a small bottle of gas next to his seat which was used to start the car when it stalled out at traffic lights. The group had the maneuver down to a science. The car would stall and everyone would go into motion. Vince would grab the gas and jump out of the car while the front seat passenger would put his foot on the gas pedal. The left rear passenger would jump out with Vince and hold the rear hood open while Vince poured some of the gas into the engine's carburetor. The front seat passenger would then turn the key and pumped the gas pedal. After a few months of this the group got together to finally rebuild the VW's engine.

The next two years of high school were filled with the things that any normal high school kid does. Saturday night football games, homecoming, the prom, running from the police; well maybe not the last one, but it was never for anything serious. High school in South Florida was not all that exciting, but there was usually always something to do so they weren't totally bored. A couple of guys even had girlfriends who would hang out and accepted that there could be one or more of the group along on a date. It was well into their senior year when the first incident involving Vince and one of the members of the group occurred.

The Cunninghams, Ken and Vince were out for a pizza one Saturday night at *Franco and Vinny's Pizza Shack* on Ft. Lauderdale beach. Jay was out on a date. He had met a girl from another school who was very attractive and wanted to "show" her off to the guys, so he came by the restaurant after their movie had let out. He really liked this girl and had tried several times to get a date with her. She had finally accepted. There was a large round table in the back corner of the restaurant where the group usually sat and tonight was no exception, so there was plenty of room for Jay and his date to join in. Vince, either being jealous or just being a jerk started in on Jay as soon as the couple sat down.

One could see that Jay was really proud of his date when he walked up and started introducing Marcie to his friends. Then he got to Vince who didn't even look up at the pair, but after they sat down Vince looked at Jay and said "Are you allowed to be eating this stuff because of your medication?" No one knew what to make of Vince's comment, but assumed it was some kind of weird joke.

Jay and Marcie had started talking with Ken when Vince interrupted their conversation. "Can you eat this stuff? I thought that if you had the clap and were taking medicine you couldn't eat spicy foods." Dave turned to Vince and in a very disapproving tone said "Vince, just shut the fuck up if that's all you got to say." Vince looked at Dave and responded "Hey, I just thought this girl would like to know what's going to happen to her when Jay knocks her up." Nobody at the table knew how to respond. That kind of talk was normal when it was just the guys, but they had never spoken that way in front of girlfriends and especially when it was someone's first date. Jay was totally embarrassed and so was Marcie. She asked to leave.

No one spoke to Vince for the rest of the night, but apparently he didn't get the hint. He continued the attack on Jay as soon as he got to school on Monday morning. Vince went around telling everyone he could find that Jay had been dumped by a girl because she found out that he had the clap. Of course the rumor spread quickly and Jay was the laughing stock of the high school. There was no rumor control which would have helped Jay out at that point, so he just had to bear it. After that incident, the group began the ostracize Vince and never really let him in on any more of the group's activities.

Amazingly, after graduation everyone remained in the area except for Vince who went away to college and out of the group's lives. Bill and Ken started attending classes at Broward Community College which was just a few miles from their homes. Dave and Nicky began working on cars, started their own Corvette shop in town and were making a go of it. Jay got himself accepted to the University of Miami, but still lived at home. Their high school days were over, but the group still stayed together and still had their Saturday night pizzas at *Franco and Vinny's*.

A couple of years went by with little change, but eventually things began to. Bill Cunningham did not really take to college and was hired by the Ft. Lauderdale Police Department as a policeman. Dave, who was always the smartest of the group, closed his business for a higher paying job with an airplane parts manufacturing company while Nicky went back to school to become a machinist. Ken stayed at BCC, but began flying and took a job as a flight instructor. Jay stuck it out and graduated college with a degree in Microbiology. Everyone in the group had lost contact with Vince, but because of what he had done to Jay, no one really cared.

It has been said that if a person has just one good friend they can consider themselves lucky. Bill, David, Jay, Nicky and Ken had been good friends for fifteen years and when anyone of the group needed help, the others were always there to lend a hand. Things continued to change, but always for the better. Dave was best man at Nicky's wedding with the others acting as groomsmen. The order was changed at Jay's wedding, but the players remained the same. The Saturday night outings were replaced with Sunday afternoon barbeques at someone's house and "cruising" the beach turned into helping out when a handyman project needed more than one set of hands. But a major change was about to happen which would play a pivotal role in all of their future lives.

Dave Cunningham was extremely smart. One might even have called him "brilliant," but there was just one problem which he could not overcome: he found school work very boring. This did not however, stop him from gaining an advanced education. He studied every engineering text book he could find and concentrated on his one true passion: automotive engineering. The entire group loved cars and in particular, racing. They went to all the major racing events in Florida every year. Florida is rich in its racing heritage with events like the Daytona 500 stock car race and the 12 Hours of Sebring sports car race. There were several drag strips and stock car tracks where the group went religiously to get their fix of racing fumes. Ken even turned a Ford Mustang he bought into a dragster and the group acted as his pit crew when he raced it. Dave took this passion to the next level and developed an idea for a revolutionary gasoline engine intake system.

As fate would have it, Dave put the finishing touches on his idea about the time of the Performance Racing Industry trade show which accompanies the Daytona 500 Race Week activities. He wanted to see if there was any interest in his idea from the racing community, so everyone packed up, tickets in hand and went to Daytona. The PRI show would be the perfect place to try to find some interest in a new idea. Every major manufacturer involved in the sport of racing had a booth at this trade show. Dave was smart enough to know that he could not give too much information away about his system, but that he would have to disclose just enough to get someone interested and possibly finance the idea.

Dave toured the trade show with the group in tow, talking to vendors and getting frustrated with what he called "their lack of vision."

The world had moved on to fuel injection, but NASCAR, the major sanctioning body in stock car racing was still running races with cars using carburetors. Dave wanted stock car racing to come up to speed as it were with modern technology. He decided to take a break from the show and they all sat down at the food court with Dave explaining the finer points of his system to the group.

After a few minutes, a gentleman approached the table and addressed Dave. "I don't mean to interrupt, but my name is Randy Butler and I could not help overhearing your conversation". Everyone at the table knew who Randy Butler was. He had been building winning race engines for the cars that competed in the American Speed Association for years and was a living legend in the sport. The ASA had produced drivers such as Alan Kulwicki and Mark Martin who had moved up to NASCAR after winning in ASA and Butler was a major engine builder for that series. Butler asked if he could sit down and hear all of Dave's idea.

Butler listened as Dave described how his system would work and how the racing sanctioning bodies could regulate the computer which was the brains of the system. Preventing cheating by the race teams was the major concern of NASCAR and the reason stock car racing had not changed over to fuel injection. They knew how to prevent cheating by regulating carburetors, but the technology behind a fuel injected powered engine was foreign to them. Dave had a simple plan and laid it all out for Butler. When Dave finished Butler said, "You know I have wanted to get stock car racing to convert over to fuel injection for a few years now. You sound like you have the answer. I would like to think about this. Can I call you when the show is over and I get back home?" Dave was almost speechless. Randy Butler was talking to him. Just some guy he had overheard talking about an off the wall idea while at the biggest racing trade show in the world. All he could manage was a "yes". Butler got Dave's number and on the Monday after the show, he followed through with his promise.

Bill Cunningham had just cleared a domestic call when the police dispatcher came over the radio and advised him to call his brother. When Dave picked up the phone he said "How cold do you think it gets in the winter in Michigan?" Bill was none too pleased about answering a worthless trivia question about weather, especially after busting his hump to get to a phone thinking there was a family emergency.

"How the hell am I supposed to know that" was the terse response to David's question. "Well Butler wants to know when I can start and what type of equipment I will need to develop a fuel injection system for racing."

Bill was now excited and said, "Are you shitting me?"

"Nope, I have to figure out how quickly I can get everything packed and up to Spring Lake, Michigan. He's sending Patty and me airline tickets to come up and find a place to stay. Mom and Dad are going to watch the kid while we're up there."

Bill was now feeling very proud of his little brother and said, "Don't worry. Find a place and we'll get you moved. I can take some time off from work if you're going to move the stuff up there yourself. Where the hell is Spring Lake anyway?"

Dave then jokingly said, "I don't know. It's somewhere on Lake Michigan, so I'll bet I freeze my balls off." In less than a month, Dave had moved his wife and son to a new home and was hard at work attempting to change the world of stock car racing.

Bill Cunningham and his brother had always been close. They were sixteen months apart and before the family moved to Florida they had lived in a rural section of northeast Ohio. Living out in the country meant that the brothers had few friends they could play with after school, so if they hadn't gotten along, they would have had no else to play with. The brothers grew up liking the same things and had many of the same interests. They particularly liked tearing apart things and putting them back together, much to the dismay of their father who more than once had to hire someone to rebuild a lawnmower. This talent would serve them both in the years to come.

After David left for Michigan, the other members of the group did not see as much of each other as they would have liked. Periodically one or more would take a trip up to Michigan, but it just wasn't the same. Ken had graduated from BCC and was now a full time pilot, flying corporate jets for a charter service out of Ft. Lauderdale

Executive Airport. Nicky had also graduated and had worked his way up to master machinist making punch and die tooling the diameter of human hairs to be used in the aerospace industry. Jay went to work as a microbiologist at St. Mary's Hospital just up the road in Riviera Beach and was working his way up to supervisor of the department.

Bill had remained a cop and after a couple of years he was transferred out of the patrol division and into the tactical squad. He was an aggressive officer while in patrol and had made several high profile arrests winning him the transfer. He started out training as a detective, investigating street level narcotics cases and once again distinguished himself with more high profile arrests. Eventually Cunningham was sent to the Miami-Dade SWAT School in Miami. This was one of the top SWAT schools in the country and the instructors taught him and the other candidates how to eliminate suspects "with great prejudice". The courses at the school taught police officers all the finer techniques of urban combat and how to overcome an aggressive suspect by any means possible. He was unknowingly developing the skills which he would be using in the future for a wholly illegal act.

Not all of Cunningham's actions while he was a police officer were without controversy. On one such occasion, he responded to an "officer needs assistance" call in which a civilian accident investigator from the department's traffic division had called for help. Cunningham and his partner, Bud Townsend were just leaving the department's parking lot when they heard a female voice, full of panic come over the police radio. "Tango 19, I need help out here! Black male wearing dark clothing just attacked a lady." The next thing they heard over the radio was the alert tone which precedes all emergency calls. This is a two second buzzing sound that is sure to get the adrenalin flowing even in the most experienced officers. The dispatcher on duty that day was experienced and not easily rattled, so in a calm, even voice she said, "Code 3, 10-94! Officer needs assistance; 1800 West Broward Boulevard. Any units in the area advise." The partners just happened to be the closest unit and answered up that they were responding. Townsend turned on the police unit's lights and siren as they raced the three blocks to the address where the accident investigator waited.

When they arrived, they were immediately confronted with a crazed black male who had struck a female passerby in the head with a chunk of concrete. As they exited their unit, the pair could see the lady lying on the side of the road in a pool of blood and saw that her assailant was rearming himself. He then began to move towards her for what they knew would be a second attack on the now helpless woman. Both officers immediately started towards the suspect, but as they did so, Cunningham found himself examining what the woman's attacker was wearing. The man looked like a World War II Navy recruiting poster. He wore a dark blue "Pea" coat complete with a double row of black buttons and a pair of dark blue bell bottom pants. Except for the "Braves" baseball cap on his head, he was right out of the 1940's.

Cunningham and Townsend had worked together for a few years, so each knew exactly what the other would do in this type of situation. Both officers moved to distract the attacker and tried to position themselves where they could disarm and arrest the man. They managed to divert his attention away from the female, but before they could react, he turned and hurled a large piece of concrete at Townsend. Cunningham did not see where Townsend had been struck, but saw him go down to the ground in a clump of weeds. Bill couldn't tell how badly Bud might have been hurt, but saw the man pick up another piece of concrete and begin to move towards his downed partner. Bill then yelled to get the man's attention as the assailant rushed towards his partner.

What occurred next happened in the blink of an eye. The man spun around and spotted Cunningham approaching. As he did, he cocked his arm back and Cunningham could see that he was holding a large piece of concrete. He knew that the man was about to let it fly in his direction. Bill saw pure hatred on the man's face and realized that he was now the target of the man's vengeance. He then realized that he was close enough to be seriously injured if the man hit his target. Cunningham had already begun to un-holster his duty weapon, but the man's actions caused him to speed up and before the man had let go of his projectile, he had leveled his weapon directly at his assailant. As the man's arm began to move forward, Bill dove to his right and at the same time pulled the trigger of his duty weapon: a Smith and

Wesson Model 19. He instinctively fired two rounds from the weapon or as his instructors had called it in training: "a double tap". As Bill hit the ground, he managed to keep his eyes on the man to see if he needed to react to any more aggression, but was somewhat puzzled by what he saw.

Every police officer mentally runs through scenarios to come up with a plan of action for different situations they might face. Cunningham was no different and had prepared himself by coming up with a plan of action for the different types of calls he thought he would encounter. A good officer will even run through different scenarios as he approaches a call, so he is mentally prepared to react if something goes wrong. Bill Cunningham however, did not possess the imagination which would have allowed him to come up with this one. Being attacked by a 1940's recruitment poster, armed with a chunk of concrete was not something he had even remotely thought he would face.

As Cunningham watched, the man just stood there in front of him with a look of confusion on his face. He did not seem to be in pain, but his facial expression indicated that he did not comprehend what was happening to him. Cunningham quickly got to his feet. As he did, he saw the man's eyes roll skyward just before he collapsed. Except for Little Bit, Bill had never actually seen anyone's reaction to being shot. He only had what he had seen on television or in the movies as a reference. The man did not respond the way Cunningham expected him to. This guy did not grab his chest with a look of pain on his face or fly backwards with his arms extended. He just stood there with that look of confusion on his face. A look that Bill knew he was never going to forget. A moment later, the man slowly fell to the ground. Cunningham did not know what to make of this, but based on the reactions of shooting victims in the movies, he had to assume that he had missed with both of his shots.

Cunningham didn't wait to see why they man collapsed. His police training took over and he reacted. He kept his weapon trained on the man as he cautiously approached him. Bill grabbed the man's left wrist and twisted it as he pulled the arm out straight from the body. He then quickly re-holstered his weapon and grabbed his handcuffs from their pouch on his utility belt. In a move that he had done many times, he slapped the cuff on the wrist he was controlling and pulled the man's arm across his back while grabbing and securing the other wrist in the cuffs. Having secured his assailant, he went to check on his partner.

Bud was just getting to his feet and had a noticeable limp as he moved towards Cunningham. The pair then went back to where Cunningham had left the man only to see that he was not moving. Bud leaned down and checked the man's pulse, but did not find one.

"Man, I think he's dead," Bud exclaimed.

"That's not possible. I missed him. You must be checking him wrong."

"No! I'm telling you, he's dead. Maybe you scared him to death."

"Bull shit! Check him again. How the hell do you scare someone to death?"

"I don't know, but I'm telling you the guy's dead."

Both officers began frantically looking for blood or anything else which might explain what was wrong with their suspect. Bud looked at Bill and said "I'm telling you there's nothing here. You scared the guy to death when you shot at him. He must have had a heart attack." Bill was only half listening as he keyed his police radio and asked the dispatcher to send EMS to the scene. Both officers then looked at each other and knew what they needed to do; they started CPR on the guy and continued until the paramedics arrived. Everything around him now sped up. EMS and the backup units all came screaming up to the scene with sirens blaring. People were now running past him, but his world had gone into slow motion.

Bill sat back on the pile of concrete his attacker had used to arm himself and watched as two paramedics worked on the lifeless body. He mindlessly glanced at his watch. The officer who was now beginning to write the report of the incident asked the dispatcher to advise the time the call was placed by the accident investigator. A second later the dispatcher came back on the radio and said, "Call received and Charlie 20 in route at 1533. EMS dispatched at 1536." Cunningham thought to himself *"How could all of that happen in just three minutes?"*

Three minutes. It took twice that long for the backup units to arrive and even longer for his supervisor and detectives to show up. He and

Bud were now surrounded by people who were asking them questions while others began talking to witnesses. Bill sat there silently staring at the yellow plastic sheet which was now covering the lifeless body he had created as other officers gathered statements and collected evidence. The lead detective on the scene grabbed Bill by the shoulder and said, "Come on, get in my car so we can head back to the station before any more of the media show up." Cunningham had not noticed them arrive, but there were now several people armed with cameras taking pictures of everything they could; including him. Bill stood up, took one last look at the yellow sheet and headed for the detective's car.

Cunningham was sitting alone in a second floor interrogation room of the Department's Detective Bureau, slowly sipping on a soda he was given by the detective who drove him back to the station. He was mindlessly staring at the can when Homicide Detective Harry Grimes walked in. Grimes was the city's senior homicide detective and Cunningham's training officer when he was still in patrol. "Hey shit head, I guess I trained you pretty good. You didn't get yourself killed out there." Bill just looked up without responding, but was happy to see that someone who had an interest in him was going to be taking his statement. "You must have spent some extra time at the range. You put both rounds into the guy," Grimes said as he pulled out a pad of paper and set up a tape recorder on the desk which was between them. Cunningham was now confused.

"You sure? I missed the guy. There was no blood."

"No, you put both rounds in his armpit. When he dropped his arm, that heavy coat must have acted as a tourniquet. The medics found the holes when they were trying to revive the guy."

"How's that even possible? You sure that's what EMS said?"

Cunningham couldn't figure out whether he should be proud of his marksmanship or not. He did know however, that the ordeal was just beginning.

The media sensationalized the story with headlines like "Police Kill Unarmed Sailor". This was only partially true. The man, Harold Timms was a merchant marine sailor who had stopped taking his medication which controlled his violent temper. They ran countless editorials about Cunningham, questioning his actions, his training and the department in general. How could an officer shoot and kill a guy throwing rocks? The newspapers never mentioned that the "rocks" were jagged chucks of concrete the size of softballs or that if Bill had been hit in the head with one he would most likely be dead right now. They also never mentioned the victim. She was a young woman who was on her way home from work and was now facing a future of pain and lost income because of one person's violent actions. No one ever found out why Timms attacked the lady on the side of the road in the first place, but she eventually recovered from her injuries. This however, took eight plastic surgery operations to get her to look the way she did before the attacks. Cunningham was forced to go through a Grand Jury investigation and was questioned for three hours over an incident which took three minutes. They finally decided not to return an indictment, but enough was enough. Bill Cunningham had made a decision of his own; this was just not worth it. It was time for a career change. He was going to look for something else to do with his life.

Chapter 3

Randy Butler had met with nothing but criticism for his idea to get stock car racing switched over to fuel injection. The "good ol' boys" didn't want anything to do with it and Randy surmised that it was because they really didn't understand it all that well. Dave's attempts to help educate them fell on deaf ears, so his project was now at a standstill. Butler had laid out a lot of money so David could develop a system that would work. The money was a secondary issue. Now, he had to lay off David after convincing him to take on the project and move up to Michigan.

"I'm really sorry about this: that it didn't work out," Randy said.

"No problem. I've learned a lot and I'm sure someone will pick me up. I can probably get a job with an Indy car or boat racing team," Dave replied.

"Why don't you try to make it on your own? The system is better than anything in the aftermarket industry and better than anything Detroit has. I'll let you have everything you've worked on as a going away present."

Dave broke the news to Bill and asked him to come up and help him move back to South Florida. He then told Bill about Butler's "gift" and suggested that they think about starting up a company to sell his system to people wanting to convert their cars from carburetors over to fuel injection. On the surface it sounded like a good idea. Street rodders, hot rodders and the marine industry were all beginning to make the switch, but they were building the systems themselves from scratch. There was no one selling a "turnkey" system that someone could just bolt to an engine and go. Dave and Bill had all they needed as far as the technology to make it work; all they really needed now was the capital to build a manufacturing plant to build them. Just a couple of million should do it, but that was a pipe dream right now because they didn't know anybody with that kind of money. Dave's idea made sense and Bill made the decision right then that there was life after police work. Now all he had to do was convince his wife that it was a good idea to leave a steady paycheck for some pipe dream.

Bill had been married for a couple of years to a girl from New York, so his wife had not been around his group of friends all that much. Bill had kept the violence that was inherent in his job at work and his wife had little knowledge of what he actually did or how violent her husband needed to be to survive in that environment. She did know however, that the stresses of the job were wearing on him. She was actually happy that he was leaving police work for a nice quiet desk job. After turning in his resignation, he put all of his efforts into finding some money for the new company. He would come up with a source, but would eventually regret the unexpected meeting which would lead to them getting the funding they needed.

A chance meeting had originally introduced the Cunninghams to Vince and another chance meeting would reunite the trio once again. Bill was just going to the Publix grocery store on Broward Boulevard to pick up some bread when he glanced over and spotted someone he thought he knew. The guy he had seen was also just walking into the grocery store and Bill hurried to catch up. Bill walked up behind the guy and said "Vince, is that you?" The man turned and Bill was now unsure if it was indeed who he thought it was. This man was seventy pounds heavier than he remembered Vince being and the once muscular frame was now soft and pudgy. His question was answered as soon as the man spoke.

"Bill, I don't believe it. How have you been? Is Dave still around?"

"Dave's fine. He just moved back here from Michigan. He was up there working, but it didn't work out. I thought you moved to New York or someplace up north."

"It was New York, but I've been back here for a few years. You still a cop?"

"No, I quit a couple of months ago. Dave and I have an idea for a business and I've been working on that. We're in the process of looking for someone to back it."

"Really! You'll have to tell me about it sometime."

Vince then handed Bill his business card saying, "Here's my number. Give me a call and the three of us will get some lunch." Bill took the card, shook Vince's hand and went to look for the bread aisle. As soon as Bill got home, he called Dave to tell him of his encounter.

A week or so went by when Bill finally placed the call to Vince. A lot of years had passed and he and his brother were not as mad at Vince as they had once been. After all, they had all been real close once and wanted to catch up with what he had been doing since he left for school. He set up a lunch date for the next day at the Bimini Boat Yard Restaurant on the 17th St. Causeway in Ft. Lauderdale.

As the brothers parked their car in the parking lot, they looked over at the valet parking area to see Vince exiting a new Mercedes Benz 560SEL sedan. Dave looked over the top of their car at Bill.

"I guess he's done OK for himself," Dave said.

"Looks that way. Wonder if he earned it legally?"

Dave just shrugged his shoulders. "Knowing Vince, there's probably a contract out on him right now."

Vince had seen the brothers approaching and waited for them to walk up before they all went in. After some small talk, the conversation turned to Vince's car.

"Did you win the lottery?" Bill said as he pointed over his shoulder at the parking lot.

"No, I started a computer business and it's going pretty good."

"I'd say so," David said.

"I sell computers through ads in computer magazines. Strictly mail order stuff. I only deal in Macs. I get them for a good price from a distributor and then sell them. No overhead, so I can sell them cheap. Make about one percent on each sale."

Bill was trying to do the math in his head. "One percent! How do you make any money?"

"Well, last year we sold over a hundred thousand units at about $850 a piece. That's how."

The conversation turned to what was good on the menu and what each had been doing over the years. They also talked about some key memories from high school and made fun of each other over some embarrassing moments that each of them would have liked to have forgotten about. Vince then brought up the subject of Dave's idea that he and Bill had talked about during their first encounter. Dave then laid out his idea, how he had developed it and how much he imagined it would cost to make the business profitable. Vince listened, but did not seem too enthusiastic about it. The trio finished lunch, exchanged phone numbers and left the restaurant promising to get together in the future. The brothers left the parking lot talking about Vince, their school days and guessing at how much Vince might now be worth.

Bill spent the next couple of weeks looking for ways to raise capital while Dave worked on refining what it would take to make the business work. Late one afternoon, Bill answered the phone and Vince was on the other end.

"When can you two come over to my office? I want you to explain your idea to my sales manager and my partner. I might be able to help out with financing this thing if they like it."

"You just tell us when and where and we'll be there."

The next day the brothers were pulling into an office park just off Griffin Road. It was similar to the many office parks in the area which housed small private businesses. Certainly not the kind of place you would expect to find a company capable of doing eight five million in sales the year before. They looked at the business signs on the front of the doors as they passed: Miller Plumbing Contractors, Data Services, Carcio Woodworking and then they spotted the one they were looking for: Compsales, LLC.

They were shown into a conference room and within a couple of minutes Vince walked in, followed by two others carrying files. Vince introduced them as Dan Bracen, his sales manager and Jim McGuire, his business partner. The brothers were somewhat surprised by Vince's excitement as he began talking to the group about Dave's idea and what he foresaw as its potential. He had not indicated anything but a passing interest in the idea at lunch, but now sounded as if it would revolutionize the industry. Vince turned to Dan and told him to show the Cunninghams what he had. Dan had already prepared an idea for a sales campaign based on Vince's description of Dave's idea. After Dan presented his ideas, Vince then turned to Jim to talk about what he had. He had put together the facts and figures of how much it would cost to put together a manufacturing operation to build the product. Vince was very grandiose in his description of what he saw in the future for Cunningham Fuel Injection Systems, Inc. He likened it to the Hughes Tool Company; they would start out with one company and expanded it to manufacture a whole line of products.

The Cunninghams left the meeting and were overwhelmed by Vince's response, particularly his proposed financial commitment to fund the entire project. They talked about having Vince as a partner and wondered if they were somehow being set up so Vince could steal Dave's ideas. They also talked about bringing in Jim as the fourth partner. They had never met him before and now Vince wanted him brought in as a partner with a twenty five percent ownership in the business. In the end, they decided that Jim would be a good partner to have. He was not flamboyant like Vince. He seemed to be the voice of reason to Vince's extravagant ideas about the business, and his ideas made good business sense. In the end, they decided not to look a gift horse in the mouth and signed a partnership agreement with Vince and Jim which would get the ball rolling.

In less than three months, they had a ten thousand square foot building in which to work. Within six months, they had leased the eight thousand square foot building next to that one and had ordered almost one million dollars' worth of manufacturing equipment. There was now a staff of twenty people working to produce Dave's idea; a self-programming computerized fuel injection system. Dan was no longer working on computer sales for Compsales; he was developing a national sales campaign which included ads in

Hot Rod, Chevy's Only and *Motor Trend* magazines as well as display booths at all the major automotive and marine tradeshows around the country. The brothers could not believe their luck and were working too hard to really examine what was happening around them. They never really questioned where the money was coming from. Vince had a successful computer sales business which they had seen for themselves, so they really didn't ask too many questions about the source of Vince's money.

It soon became apparent that Vince was a micromanager. He insisted on daily meetings and wanted to control what projects the designers were working on, even though he had no background in design work. It was also evident that he was becoming more agitated as engineering and production issues delayed the product's unveiling. He became condescending and even hostile in meetings and began threatening even the brothers with termination if his schedules were not met. Those who had a background in this type of work wrote it off to Vince not understanding the design process and how complicated it could be. Bill saw it as something different. It might have been the instincts he developed as a police officer, but he knew there was something under the surface which Vince was not disclosing.

The product was finally released for sale and most of the major magazines carried articles about the revolutionary systems which not only produced more horsepower, but saved gas in the process. Sales were beginning to come in, but not at the rate Vince wanted. The company was moving forward with its marketing plan which included regular attendance at different trade shows. This of course meant a lot of traveling around the country.

Vince, who was now trying to run two businesses, wanted to be at all the shows, but did not want to waste time in airports. He started to look at chartering airplanes which would run on his schedule. Dave suggested using the company Ken Martin worked for. Why not get Ken involved so he could make some money instead of some other pilot they didn't know was Dave's reasoning. Vince began chartering private jets to get him around the country to the various shows. He was dropping huge amounts of money to charter jets, but spending money never seemed to bother Vince. Attendance at the trade shows was working and sales began to increase, but still not at the rate Vince wanted. He continued to yell and make threats. Everyone was now dreading the morning meetings and listening to Vince's rampages.

Jim, who lived in Los Angeles, was now commuting less and less to Florida. He made it to several of the trade shows the company attended and had long conversations on the phone with both Bill and Dave, but limited his conversations with Vince. More than once Vince could be heard behind closed doors yelling at Jim over the phone about issues with Compsales. After one such phone call, Vince called everyone into his office. "This is not open for questions. Jim McGuire is no longer connected with me or any of my businesses. He's been stealing from the company and I've taken his stock away. I now own fifty percent of Cunningham and we're making some changes around here." Like everyone else in the office, Bill and Dave were stunned. Jim stealing money from the company was something they never would have imagined. They stayed behind after everyone else left Vince's office. They wanted an explanation.

"Jim has been stealing money from Compsales and I have to cover the losses from my own money. There's not going to be a lot of extra cash, so you two will have to either come up with some money or pledge your stock to cover a loan from me."

"Wait, I don't understand. You will now loan the company money if we give you our stock?" Dave asked.

"That's right. You want to stay in business. I get your stock and you get a stock option. You get your stock back after I get paid off."

"You already have that agreement. You accepted twenty five percent of the stock for financing the company. Dave and I have worked our asses off, developed a product which we now have patents on and you don't think that's worth anything?"

Vince's face was now blood red and he was now leaning over his desk, yelling and pointing his finger at Dave. "Here's the bottom line. If you want to stay, you'll give up your stock. The company owns the patents and I own fifty percent of the business now. I'll just close the doors and since I'm the major creditor; I'll get the patents and go ahead without you. Now I've got work to do. You'll have the papers to sign in the morning."

The brothers just looked at each other and left Vince sitting in his office. They went to Dave's office, but Bill said, "Come on. Let's get out of here and go somewhere where we can talk without anyone listening in." They got in Dave's car and went to a coffee shop down the road from their office. They sat down and ordered a couple of sodas.

"Something's not right. He said he just found out about Jim stealing money, but he already has stock options ready to go for us to sign. Those would take several days to draw up. We need to call Jim and get his side of the story," Bill said while trying to control his anger over the situation.

"You're right. He's up to something. We need to find out what it is before we sign anything."

"We also need to find out a little more about Compsale and see why he gets such good deals," Dave said.

They went to Bill's home and placed a call to Jim. Bill was only able to get "Hey Jim" out of his mouth when Jim said, "You guys know me. I didn't steal anything. Vince is pulling a fast one; he's not only out to get control of Compsale, he wants to take control of Cunningham from you two."

"Jim, Dave and I both know that there has been something going on, but we want your side of the story."

"It's real simple. Vince has been avoiding paying his supplier for the computers to fund Cunningham. When sales began to slow down, his supplier was able to catch up with their billing and found that Vince owed them almost a million in past due bills. He covered his ass by saying that I had embezzled the money which was owed to Compsales's creditors ."

"So he doesn't have all the money he claims? He's been bullshitting us all along," Bill asked in disbelief.

"Kind of. He had enough money to fund Cunningham if he had managed it properly, but he wants to be another Howard Hughes. He spent way more than he had budgeted for and it took longer than he figured to get sales going."

"How did it take so long for his supplier to figure he owed them so much?"

"Vince is not a legitimate dealer. He's grey market."

"What the hell is that," Dave asked from the other phone.

"He has someone on the inside who adds his computers to a legitimate order. In this case, it's a company called Caribbean Trading. They get an order for five thousand computers from a legitimate dealer; this insider then adds Vince's order for say three thousand more. Vince gets a discount which he would not normally get. He gets the same discount as the stores with overhead which he doesn't have. He then can sell for less than they do. The inside guy then plays with the billing until Vince sends in the money."

Bill's concern showed in his voice. "Where do we stand then?"

"Vince hid the bills from me. When I found out what he was doing he got pissed off and said that he was blaming me for stealing company funds. He said that if I didn't want to cover Compsales bills myself, he would make me pledge my stock until he paid the bill or he would close the business."

"That's the same shit he's pulling on us," Dave said.

"Jim, we need to think this over and come up with a plan. We'll call you tomorrow," Bill said.

The next day Vince met the brothers as they walked in the door. "I've got your new contracts. I need them signed now." Both Bill and Dave walked past Vince and entered Dave's office without saying a word to him. This seemed to really irritate Vince. He followed them into the office and slammed the door behind him. Vince then threw the contracts on Dave's desk and sat down.

Dave looked at the papers, then at Vince.

"We talked to Jim last night and his story really doesn't match yours."

"I don't give a shit what Jim said to you yesterday. If you want to keep this business, you'll sign the papers."

"We know about Caribbean Trading and how you lied to them about Jim," Bill said.

"Once again, I don't give a shit. You can come up with some money or get out."

"Do you really think that without Dave's expertise and his status in the industry, you're going to be able to sell anything," Bill added.

"I can get people in here to do exactly that."

"So when *Hot Rod* magazine calls and they can't get Dave on the phone, what do you think they're going to say, Hey, the guy who invented the stuff is no longer at Cunningham's, but let's buy their stuff anyway. You're not dealing in reality," Bill said.

"You're screwing Jim and now you're screwing us. I would also imagine that this company is in financial trouble also. You've been falsifying the books here too, haven't you?" David asked.

Vince didn't address that question. He just said, "You can either sign or get out."

Dave didn't respond to Vince. He picked up an empty box that was in his office and began putting the pictures of his family that were on his desk into it. Vince did not say a word, got up and left the office. Bill looked at Dave and said, "I guess we had better find a lawyer." He then headed off to his office to see if he had an empty box too.

The lawsuit took months to settle and in the end Vince paid the Cunninghams a fraction of what their stock was worth. They had not wanted to settle, but by this time Dave had discovered he had a medical problem. He had colon cancer and it was advanced. A court trial might possibly take years to settle and he needed to take care of his family, so they decided to take the first reasonable offer Vince made. This it itself would prove difficult to do. Vince had learned of Dave's cancer and tried to use this to his advantage. He tried to stall the process as much as possible hoping Dave would succumb to his disease, but luckily the Cunningham's had a no nonsense attorney who was able to get them an offer they could live with.

Dave's death had upset Bill beyond words. Dave had been his best friend since they were born. The two had done everything together for as long as Bill could remember. All the joking, kidding around and even crying together was now gone. It took a long time for Bill to come to grips with the fact that Dave was no longer there. More than once, he picked up the phone to call Dave after seeing an article or something on television he knew his brother would like only to realize that he was no longer there. Bill and his wife, Laura continued to have cookouts and celebrate holidays with Dave's wife and kids, but it just was never going to be the same. There was now a huge hole in Bill's life which he was convinced would not be there had everything worked out differently with Vince.

While all of the drama at the business was going on, Vince had failed to pay the company's debts which included the one to the air charter company. The charter service's owners knew that Vince and Ken were once friends and even though they couldn't prove it, they assumed that Ken had made some sort of deal with Vince so he would not have to pay them for their services. Ken lost his job because of it. Jim didn't make out any better. He had no real recourse against Vince. Caribbean Trading bought Vince's story and he made good on his debts to them, gaining all of Jim's stock in Compsale in the process. Jim's reputation in the computer industry was ruined, but he could not sue Vince because the owners of Caribbean Trading were not willing to testify against Vince who was one of their biggest customers. Every one of these people, who had once viewed Vince as a friend, now had a reason to hate him. Dave's death not long after the lawsuit was settled was the spark that caused Bill to develop his plan. In order to succeed, the plan would need the individual talents of those Vince had alienated.

CHAPTER 4

A couple of months after Dave's death, Jim called Bill. Jim wanted to meet Bill in Las Vegas to "unwind, decompress and have some laughs" as Jim put it. Bill had not yet found a new job and didn't have anything else to do, so he decided to take Jim up on his offer. Both had become very familiar with Las Vegas. They had spent the last couple of years participating in the Specialty Equipment Market Association trade show which was held in Vegas every fall. The S.E.M.A. show was the largest aftermarket automotive trade show in the world and Cunningham had a large booth in the show. The four partners had once had a good time there. Now it would be just the two of them. They decided before going that the past would not be brought up, but inevitably it was.

It was late one evening that involved too much drinking. Jim and Bill sat in a quiet section of the Mizuya Lounge at the Mandalay Bay Hotel. They knew this was one of the best places in Vegas to get sushi and they sat talking about old times in between bites of Ika and Mirugai. Jim took a drink of his Ashai beer and said, "I wish Dave was here to enjoy this. He really liked to come here." Bill didn't answer, but he silently made the same wish. They were both quiet for a minute, reminiscing about their past experiences in Vegas when Jim made a comment which gave Bill the opening he was looking for.

"I wish there was something we could do to get back at that bastard," Jim said. Bill knew exactly who Jim was referring to. Bill leaned over close to Jim so his voice would not be overheard and said, "Maybe there is." The expression on Jim's face became more serious as he said, "What do you want to do, kill him." Bill's look gave away his thoughts.

Jim sat for a moment and said, "Are you kidding. You really want to kill him?"

"Do you know anyone who deserves it more?"

"Do you actually have a plan or are you just talking?"

"Not now. Not here. We'll talk about this later," Bill answered.

The pair sat quietly, saying little as they finished the last of their beers, but each was mentally picturing the results of what they had just discussed. They paid for their meal and said their good-nights. They planned to have breakfast in the morning before heading to the airport and then back home.

The next morning, Jim was already at a table when Bill came into the restaurant. Bill slid into the booth and before he even got settled Jim asked, "Were you serious last night or was it the beer?"

"I was serious."

"I know you were a cop and all, but can it be done without getting caught? Would you do it or are you talking about getting someone to do it for you?"

"You never bring someone in you don't know. You start talking to someone and the guy who you think you're hiring to do a job turns out to be an undercover cop. It needs to be kept in house."

"Do you already have a plan? One that will work."

"I've got an outline. I need to work out some things, but I will need some help covering my tracks. I have to know if you're in and serious about this."

"The bastard took away my business, my reputation and one of my best friends. Yes, I'm serious. What do you have so far?"

"I need to make sure Vince is at a certain spot and a specific time. I have a basic idea of what I want to do. I want to create the deal of the century for Vince, so he is willing to follow instructions instead of dictating the situation. I want to use his greed against him to get him to do what I want."

"Vince is a greedy bastard. Just make it a deal he can't pass up. You just tell me what you want me to do," Jim said.

"Like I said, I have to work on learning a few things. It's going to take me awhile to get things set up so don't think I've changed my mind if you don't hear from me right away. Might be months before I'm ready. I also need to convince someone else we're going to need to help us. This person is crucial to making the plan work. We can then get back together when everything is in place and I will lay out the whole thing for you."

They changed the subject, but the idea of making Vince pay was still in their minds when they left the restaurant and shared a taxi to the airport. Jim was going to play a key role in Bill's plan, but there were three more members who would be just as important if this was going to work.

Bill managed to talk the reservations clerk at the Delta Airlines counter into putting him in an aisle by himself. The plane was less than half full, but she acted as if she was doing him a huge favor. He wanted to be able to work on the outline of his plan without having to endure making small talk with a person in the seat next to him who felt like talking for the entire five hour flight home. He had a basic idea of what it would take and how he was going to do it; he just needed to lay it out on paper so he could see it.

He settled into his seat for the ride home and took out his notebook. In it, he made a list of topics skipping down several lines between each new topic; Location, Weapon, Ammunition, Surveillance, Escape and Alibi. Each topic was then subdivided into categories; listing things he already knew and the skills or information he needed to obtain. He also listed the people he would need to help him and a description of their role. Cunningham would plan each part in such a way that if they were questioned by the police, his partners would not have to lie and still not give away any of the plan. He did make one notation in the notebook which applied to everyone; no phones calls discussing anything to do with the shooting except on the phones he would supply them. As the plane touched down at Ft. Lauderdale International Airport, Cunningham made sure to put all of his notes away in his backpack. He could just imagine the questions he would face if they were left behind and fell into the hands of some nosy cop.

CHAPTER 5

Jay Goldman had always wanted to be a cop, but his parents had pushed him in another direction. They had wanted him to be a doctor, but settled for him getting his PhD in microbiology. When he had the opportunity to become a reserve police officer with the City of Plantation, he jumped on it. After graduating from the reserve academy, Jay worked his way up to the point where he was allowed to man a patrol car by himself. He usually worked one day a week on the weekends and loved it. Bill Cunningham's house happened to be in Jay's patrol area, so he stopped by regularly.

Jay parked his patrol car in the circle driveway in front of Bill's house and spotted him in the yard as he was getting out of his car.

"Hey, where have you been? I stopped by last weekend, but Laura said you were gone," Jay said as he walked across Bill's freshly cut lawn.

"I went out to see Jim in Vegas. I spent a few days with him."

"Did you win anything or lose as usual?"

"Lost, but had a good time doing it," Bill said as he pushed his lawn mower back into his garage. He then motioned for Jay to follow him into the house. Bill had wanted to talk to Jay about his plan and figured now would be a good time to feel Jay out to see if he would help. Cunningham was fairly sure that he already knew how Jay would react to what he was about to ask him to do.

Laura was out shopping so Bill knew he could talk freely to Jay and not worry about explaining to his wife what he had in mind. Even though she hated Vince as much as he did, he was still unsure how she would feel about her loving husband shooting someone in cold blood. She had been through a lot with him, but this might be pushing it.

Bill had always thought that he would be a lifelong bachelor. He had dated some really nice women, but the relationships would only last a few months. He was okay with this because there were always women who wanted to date a police officer. The women would find it exciting until Bill's uncertain schedule or the stress of the job would end the relationship. Bill was in his late thirties when a friend set him up on a blind date with Laura. The first one he had even been on. They hit it off right away. He proposed and she accepted on their four date. They were married six months later. She had been with him when he was involved in his shooting and supported him when he left the department and faced an uncertain future. She was even supportive when he passed up a secure well paying job to start up a business with Dave and Vince. He knew she loved him dearly, but he had not yet decided if he would ever tell her what he had done once the deed was done.

Jay had followed Bill into the kitchen. Cunningham handed Jay one of the two glasses of cold water he had just poured. "I want to talk to you about something." Jay examined Bill's face as he accepted the water and realized that whatever they were about to discuss was serious. "OK, what's going on? Why so serious," Jay said, taking a sip of water while sitting down at the kitchen table.

Bill sat down at the table across from Jay. "I've come up with an idea which both Jim and I are going through with, but I need your help."

"Whatever it is, I'm in," Jay said immediately.

"Well, before you commit I need to tell you what it is," Bill said as he leaned closer and lowered his voice as if someone were listening in on their conversation.

"What's up? You planning to kill someone?" Jay asked sarcastically. He then saw the expression on Bill's face change and realized that was exactly what Bill was about to admit to. Bill realized that his expression had given him away and there was now no turning back. He just needed to be sure that if Jay didn't want to help, he would simply keep what he knew to himself.

"Vince has screwed Jim and me over, and Dave is no longer here because of him. He's been screwing over people for as long as we have known him. Remember that night at the pizza shack?"

"I know, but kill him?" Jay said.

"I need your help. You are not going to be directly involved. All I need you to do is to be working the day I plan to do this."

"What do you mean by "you do it"?" Jay asked.

"I've got a plan that is still in the works. Jim is on board and there are a couple of things I need to learn before I go through with it. I'm not going to start it until I'm sure it will work. It may take time, so just chill and I will fill you in when the time comes."

The two sat silently for a few moments while each digested what the other had said. Bill examined Jay's expression as he mulled over what he had just heard and was now confident that Jay wouldn't report this conspiracy to the authorities. He also knew that Jay would keep it to himself if he didn't agree to help.

Jay sat staring at his glass of water and began running his fingers over the droplets of water which had formed on the outside of the glass. As he did this, he began developing a mental picture of the plan's aftermath. Jay had also blamed Vince for Dave's death and was upset over the brothers losing their business. Most of all, Jay still never forgave Vince for that night at the restaurant. He had spent a lot of time wondering what would have happened between him and Marcie had Vince not acted like a jerk that night.

Jay sat quietly for a few moments then said, "Tell me what you need me to do."

Bill laid out the basics and made a point to tell Jay that he would not be jeopardizing anything by helping out with the plan. If Jay followed the plan, no one would ever know his involvement. Now all Bill needed to do was convince two more people to help. One would be a key player because he would be supplying an alibi for those who might come under investigation by the police. Ken Martin had all the same reasons for wanting Vince dead and his experience as a pilot would give the group the alibi they needed to avoid prosecution. Bill set up a meeting with Ken.

It was easy to convince Ken to become part of the plan. The air charter business in South Florida is a small community and what had happened with the company Ken had worked for soon became common knowledge. Vince's punishment would be that he could no longer charter a plane from anyone, but Ken was also being punished. He was having a hard time finding another flying job because of Vince's actions. Ken's participation in the plan would be a simple one. All he needed to do was to get to Vegas and pretend to be Bill for a few hours. Like Jay, all Ken had to do was follow Bill's plan and he would not have to lie to the police about his involvement. Well maybe just adjust the truth a little, but not to the extent that even an experienced detective would pick up on it.

Bill had told each one he had talked to that he would lay out the entire plan for their review after he had completed it. He was not going to rush the planning stage and possibly over- look something that would lead investigators to them. He was sure that due to their past involvement with Vince, the police would be asking them questions, but if the plan was thought out properly, the police would have nothing to connect the group to Vince's death. After he was sure that he had all the players lined up, he made a phone call.

"The people I need are all on board," Bill said.

"When do you plan to do this?" was the response from the voice on the other end.

"I need to figure out a couple of things. Might be awhile."

"OK, I've waited this long, I guess a while longer won't make a difference."

"I don't want to rush this and make a mistake. You have as much to lose as any of us. I told you when you first got in touch with me that it could take up to a year to get this done. You need to stay patient and remember what's at the end of the tunnel. All you need to do is make the changes we talked about."

"How will I know when you're ready? I can't just leave this phone on and wait for your call."

"Jim agreed that the business idea would work. We'll set up the business meeting like we talked about and get Vince to be where I want him at the right time. I won't be contacting you from here on out, but you'll know when the plan is moving forward. You just make sure you follow up and do what you're supposed to do."

"Are you sure you can trust these guys?"

"None of them liked Vince and I grew up with all of them. They won't let us down." Cunningham hung up and began to go over the plan again. He had noted two important skills he would need if he was going to pull this off. He was very good with a hand gun, but did not have much experience with rifles. All throughout his police career, he had been trained on different types of weapons and became very good with all of them. The weapons he trained on however were primarily for close-in combat. He needed the experience of a sniper. He needed to develop the ability to reach out and touch his target from a long way off. Bill also needed to learn ballistics and how bullets would react traveling through different objects.

Cunningham had been unemployed since his settlement with Vince. He had received a fair amount of money when he left the police department when they paid him for his accumulated sick time and unused vacation. He had put that money into an emergency account which he had not had to go into yet. He and Dave settled with Vince for a little over $50,000 each, but he had gone through most of that trying to support his family. He needed to find a job. His wife worked and luckily they had not started a family yet. His wife's income helped, but they would have to make some lifestyle changes and soon if he didn't find a job.

Bill spent his days looking for a job and refining his plan. He had not mentioned to his wife anything of what he was planning and he never would. She would come into his den to check on him and see all the notes he had been compiling sitting on the desk. She just assumed he was doing research for the different jobs he was applying for. What she didn't know was the type of jobs he was researching.

A major point of Cunningham's plan was to avoid any connection between what he needed to learn and the plan itself. He would not be able to enroll in a civilian sniper school without there being a record of his enrollment. He knew that the investigators would look into Vince's background and scrutinize anyone who had a grudge with him. It would not look too good if a person who had a major problem with Vince in the past had just attended a sniper school, especially when Vince was taken out by a long range shot. He found the solution to this problem and his employment issue in much the same way he had gotten involved with any of this in the first place: by chance.

Bill Lundky had gone to the police academy with Bill and had left the department shortly after Cunningham. Lundky had gone to work for a company called Securicorp who was doing security work in Iraq. There were simply not enough military units available to provide protection for all of the companies who were now involved in rebuilding Iraq after the U.S. invasion, so the government turned to private security companies. These companies supplied security personnel to protect civilian and military installations as well as protecting the civilian and military personnel who worked within them. Lundky had heard that Bill was looking for a job and gave him a recruiter's number to contact. Cunningham had done a little research of his own and found out that the people who worked for these companies had a wide range of specialized training; some he knew he would need to learn in order to complete his plan.

Unlike the common misconception about these companies, the people hired to fill this role were not mercenaries, but soldiers who had fought in the Iraq war or police officers with tactical experience. Bill had the skill set that the recruiter was looking for and he soon found himself on the Securicorp payroll. Now all he had to do was explain to his wife why he had left police work only to end up doing the same type of work in a war zone.

CHAPTER 6

Laura Cunningham had little time to complain. Her husband had filled out the application on Tuesday, talked to the recruiter on Wednesday, filled out the contract on Thursday and was on his way to training at Fort Bliss in El Paso, Texas on Saturday. Two weeks later, his plane was touching down at the BIAP; the Baghdad International Airport. Cunningham had been hired to run PSD (Personal Security Detail) missions in and around the city of Baghdad which put him out in the dangerous part of the city on a regular basis.

Laura had of course not wanted to see Bill leave. She would now have to take care of things at home. It now fell on her to cut the grass and fix things when they broke, but this really did not bother her as much as spending time apart from the person she loved. The fact that he was now making almost four times what he did as a cop made her being alone almost worth it. Bill had noticed that during their almost daily phone conversations that her demeanor changed when the paycheck hit the bank. They often joked about how cheerful she was every other Friday. The one good thing was that Bill trusted Laura with all that money he was making off the taxpayers who were funding the United States State Department's efforts in Iraq. Laura knew how to stretch a dollar. He referred to her as a reincarnated accountant. She was investing their money and doing a really good job at it. If his eventual plan did not work out the way he had hoped, she would still be set for life if he was no longer in the picture.

Bill had lied to his wife about his job and what he would be doing when he left for Iraq. He told her that he would be based in the "Green

Zone" which was a one mile by two mile walled off compound located in the heart of the Baghdad. The "Green Zone" housed the U.S. embassy, other coalition embassies and an assortment of private and military compounds. He knew what he was getting into, but the term "Green Zone" made the place sound safe and he did not want to unduly worry his wife. When Laura did ask, "is it safe there?" Bill would always reply, "Yes, as far as you know". What she did not need to know was that the area was hit with daily rocket and mortar attacks or attacked by suicide bombers who hit the "Green Zone" checkpoints on a regular basis.

As soon as Cunningham stepped off the plane, he realized that he had stepped into a world he had never experienced before. The first thing Bill noticed was that every building, road, or anything else of any importance was surrounded by a temporary ten foot high wall made up of concrete sections known as "T-Walls". As he traveled the eight mile road which connected the BIAP and the "Green Zone", he saw the aftermath of the U.S. invasion. There were bombed out cars, buses, homes and businesses lining the road which had the military designation of "Route Irish". As disturbing as this sight was, Cunningham was more concerned about the more recent evidence of insurgent attacks along the road. There were craters and the burnt shells of military and civilian vehicles which were the result of IED's or Improvised Explosive Devices which were placed alongside the roadway and remotely detonated. There was also evidence of the almost daily rocket attacks which were fired at the "Green Zone" from the surrounding neighborhoods.

After a couple of hours of orientation, Cunningham was assigned to a team and found himself sitting in an armored Chevrolet Suburban, heading back to the BIOP to pick up some VIP who had just flown in. This was the end of summer and even with the vehicle's air conditioner set on max, he was still sweating. The fact that he was wearing fifty pounds of equipment, consisting of a bullet proof vest, ammunition and flash bangs might have had something to do with his discomfort. As the three-vehicle convoy sped along "Route Irish", Bill scanned the houses, apartment buildings and overpasses from the back seat of the vehicle looking for anything that might do them harm. It was common for insurgents to drop mortar shells or hand grenades off the overpasses at passing convoys. For this reason, convoys operated at high speed and frequently changed lanes, particularly when they drove under an overpass. This eight to ten minute trip got the adrenaline pumping, but after a few weeks it all became very common place.

It had all become very routine to Cunningham. He lived in a walled compound where nothing changed. The buildings were all surrounded by T-Walls and sand bags as well as the walkways which give the impression that one was walking in a canyon. The days he wasn't working became very monotonous. There were restaurants and even bars within the "Green Zone", but each night he saw the same group of people at the same places. Even getting shot at or experiencing the blast of a mortar round had become commonplace. IED's were always a threat along any road around Baghdad which was being used by coalition forces. Bill reasoned that the odds of getting hit by one was roughly the same as getting killed in an accident on I-95 in South Florida, so he didn't worry about them very much.

Several of the friends Bill had made while in Baghdad all lived in a section of the Embassy compound called "Camp Travis". The camp was named for an army PFC who had been killed during the Iraq war and consisted of row after row of living quarters. This housing or "hooch's" as they were called, consisted of metal conex shipping containers that had been converted into small two man apartments. Each conex had sand bags covering the outside walls and roof and the entire compound was surrounded by "T" walls. There was not much to do at night, so the group converted one corner of the camp into an outdoor seating area, using ammunition boxes for seats and camouflage netting as a sun shade. They tried to make it as comfortable as possible. Someone had put up Christmas lights along the "T" walls and speakers were mounted to the walls with the wires running back into one of the hooch's where they were connected to a stereo. There was even a palm tree strung with holiday light in a planter located in one of the corners.

After dinner, several of the friends would break out the coolers full of beer and sit around talking about the missions they had that day or what they were going to do on leave. No one ever got to the point of being drunk, but drinking a few beers made relaxing just that much easier.

One night during the summer proved to be a little more exciting than usual. The sun had set and the temperature had dropped from its daytime high of a hundred and twenty degrees to a more comfortable ninety or so. The groups had just settled into their usual seats and were getting comfortable when they heard the "Duck and Cover" alarm sounded. This is a system which is able to monitor incoming rockets or mortars, giving people inside the compound a few seconds to try to protect themselves. This particular alarm was followed almost immediately by a mortar shell exploding a couple of hundred feet from them.

Each member of the group looked at one another, as they tried to figure out what their next move would be. It didn't take long for them to decide what their next move was going to be. The second explosion, this time just a hundred feet or so away had them all jumping up and running for a concrete bunker which was just outside their patio area. The third explosion blew a large cloud of dust and debris into the bunker just as the last person dove in for cover. Even though they were now choking on the fine Iraqi sand which filled the air inside the bunker, they decided to wait to see what would happen next before exiting.

After a minute or two they left the bunker, covered with sand and still coughing from the dust. After a quick head count which revealed that everyone was accounted for, they went to return to their seats only to find out that their seats were now missing along with everything else on the patio. The mortar had scored a direct hit, leaving a good size hole and a lot of busted up lumber behind. The worst part was that the mortar appeared to have made a direct hit on their beer cooler, which pissed them off even more than they already were. It took a couple of weeks, but the patio was put back together and the beer cooler was restocked.

Cunningham however, was not going to worry much about this interruption to his social life. In between his missions, he devoted a lot of time to studying and asking questions which would help him meet his goal. He had quickly become efficient in the use of the Colt Defense M4A1 carbine while training in Texas. This weapon was his main form of defense in Iraq, but he was now surrounded by people who had an extensive knowledge of all forms of weaponry. He had no problem getting the information he needed. No one in this environment questioned why he was so inquisitive about weapons or why he needed to know what would be the most effective means of killing someone.

Cunningham went to the rifle range every chance he got. He made friends with people who were ex-military snipers and had them teach him what he needed to learn. He learned how to adjust a weapon by factoring in such variables as ballistic coefficient, temperature, wind, angle to the target, spin drift, and about a dozen other variables that would affect bullet flight over long distances. He then began to practice hitting targets at ever longer distances. Bill became very proficient with this new skill, but using this new talent in an urban setting and against a car instead of a paper target would involve some specialized practice back home.

One of the benefits of working in the "Green Zone" was meeting people from all over the world. One group in particular interested Bill. They were canine handlers from South Africa whose job it was to conduct searches for explosives, but that is not why Cunningham was interested in the group. They were all big game hunters who had a lot of experience with different types of ammunition. He had seen firsthand as a police officer how unpredictable the trajectory of a bullet became when it went through a vehicle windshield. The bullet would either be deflected or become fragmented. Neither case would fit his needs. He had seen one incident where officers had fired nine rounds through the front windshield at a suspect who was shooting at them and all had missed their mark. The windshield had caused the bullets to change their flight path as they passed through the glass. He wanted to determine what type of bullet would do its job and not be deflected or fragment once it passed through the glass.

Cunningham learned from the South Africans that a solid bullet which happened to be banded in the U.S. would do the trick. It had great penetration power and was used for dangerous game. According to Johann Swinepoxes, the K-9 supervisor and their most experienced hunter; "this .308, 168 grain round should do the trick mate". He even offered to get Bill as many boxes of the ammunition he wanted the next time he went on leave to South Africa. Of course, Johann thought he was giving advice on shooting an insurgent in a fleeing vehicle and not for what Bill had in mind.

Bill was not worried about receiving the promised ammunition. No one ever checked their luggage coming into Iraq, it was getting it back to the states that he needed to worry about. The ammunition was illegal in the states and Bill was sure there would be some sort of federal smuggling changes attached if he was caught. He had heard numerous stories about guys shipping home questionable items. These included guns, Iraqi souvenirs and even one guy who managed to ship back a solid gold toilet from Saddam Hussein's bathroom. It was rumored that he now owed a very nice cattle ranch somewhere in Montana. Bill worked on the problem and eventually found an enterprising airman who would smuggle the boxes back to the states on the C-130 aircraft he was assigned to. This of course, came with a price tag which was not too unreasonable. He would just tell Laura not to open the box when it arrived unless she wanted to ruin her Christmas present.

Cunningham's daily routine rarely changed. On the days he was assigned to work, he would be up around four in the morning. Bill would dress, get breakfast and head over to the briefing room to get the information on the day's run. One the days he was off, his choice of entertainment was limited. It was either the gym, bootlegged movies on CD's or television from India which only seemed to broadcast rugby games or professional dart championships from England. To say the least, it was really boring not to be working.

Cunningham did not like to be bored, so he ran as many missions as possible. On the days Bill worked, he and his team members would go after their briefing to check out their assigned vehicles and make sure their weapons were in working order. They would then go and pick up the State Department civilians they were assigned to. The "principles" or "Blue Badgers" as they referred to them as were then loaded into the vehicles and given a quick briefing on what they needed to do should the shit hit the fan. The team would then drive the Blue Badgers to whatever meeting they were having that day or to the BIOP if they were heading home for a vacation. The team's job was to make sure nothing happened to the "principle". Getting a Deputy Ambassador "greased" while you were protecting them does not look good on your resume, so everyone on the team took their job seriously.

These missions would often take Bill outside the relative safety of the "Green Zone". They would run mission into town on roadways with code names such as "Irish" or "Freedom". These roadways came complete with bad guys who would shoot at the convoys from rooftops or drop explosives down on the vehicles from overpasses. The vehicles were all "up armored" which is to say they were specially built with armor plating to protect the occupants.

The real danger did not usually come from small arms fire, but from bombs which were either concealed in vehicles or planted alongside the roadway. Everyone on the team would look for anything out of the ordinary while out on the road. A vehicle parked on the shoulder or a pile of rocks close to the edge could be a hiding place for explosives. These bombs were remotely detonated using cell phones so the al-Qaeda operatives did not have to be in the area and risk harm to themselves.

It would be amazing to most observers that people who worked in this type of violent environment would have a sense of humor and make jokes about their job. Cunningham was however, use to the dark humor. He had learned from being a cop that joking about situations that most would find appalling was a form of stress release and a way to keep from going insane over the carnage one sees on a daily bases.

Bill's phone conversations with his wife were about everything except his job. She had for the most part, stopped watching the news for fears that she would see him on the news one night dead or mangled. She tried to keep these feelings out of her voice during their phone calls and it killed her not to ask questions about what he did. He on the other hand was not going to unduly add any more stress on her than she already felt, so their conversations were about things they would do when he got home. This system of denial from both of them seemed work, but things changed one day while Bill was on his way to the airport to pick up someone coming in from the states.

After one morning briefing, Bill's team went out to the vehicle staging area only to find that one of their team's warped sense of humor had manifested its self in the form of a large red bull's-eye which had been painted on the rear door of their sport utility vehicle. The rear gunner, more commonly known as the "trunk monkey" explained that everyone kept shooting at the convoy but never hit anything. He was giving them a target to aim at. The team naturally thought this was funny and proceeded to have a team picture taken by the artwork. Bill having a moment of bad judgment sent the picture to his wife.

The team then loaded up and headed to the airport. Their three vehicle team was following another convoy on Route Irish when all hell broke loose. A Rocket Propelled Grenade or RPG hit the last vehicle in the front convoy. This was followed by machine gun fire from several high rise apartment buildings which lined the roadway. The front convoy had a civilian with them so they ran for the safety of the airport while Bill's team stopped to rescue the contractors in the damaged SUV.

Everyone's adrenalin rate was up as they exited their vehicles and took cover behind the SUV's. Each member had their weapons pointed towards the apartments looking for targets in an attempt to protect the team's medic who was now caring for the injured. There was however, no need to return the gun fire. As usual, the attackers immediately fled so they did not put themselves in jeopardy. The two contractors in the damaged vehicle were not badly hurt and were helped into one of the team's SUV. Cunningham's team then headed for the safety of the airport. Bill's return trip back to the "Green Zone" was uneventful and after securing their equipment the team headed straight for their little oasis and a cold beer.

Bill sipped a beer as he sat with his back against a "T" wall and listen to some of the team's younger members relive the events of the day. Cunningham was older than most of the guys he worked with and was over wasting time reliving such events. He had been in similar situations most of his professional life. If it wasn't some religious nut on Route Irish it had been a drug dealer on the streets of Fort Lauderdale trying to do him in. He knew from experience that you react first and worry about it later. As with any profession which faces danger, especially ones where harm to one's self comes quickly and unexpectedly, a person will find themselves reacting almost without thinking. They rely on their training to get them through the tuff situation and generally do not think about how dangerous the situation was until after the fact. Policeman, fireman and serviceman in combat experience this on a regular basis. It's after things calm down and the danger is over that the "oh shit" moment happens.

Cunningham was on his second beer and had tuned out the younger guys when his phone rang. He was enjoying the quiet and was not going to answer the phone until he looked at the caller ID and saw that the call was from his wife.

"Hi wife," Bill said sounding a little happier than normal.

"You son of a bitch! What the hell are you doing over there?"

Bill was a little confused by the response. How is the hell did he manage to piss off his wife from eighty five hundred miles away? He quickly got up from his seat and walked to a place where his conversation would not be overheard by the others.

"What's wrong?" Bill asked almost sleepily.

"You told me you worked in the Green Zone."

"I do. As a matter of fact I'm sitting outside my hooch having a beer right now."

"Then why is it I see that damn SUV with the red bulls-eye out on a road getting shot at on TV? The news headline was government contractors in firefight in Baghdad, more after the break."

Cunningham's mind was now racing trying to come up with a reasonable explanation that his wife would buy. It needed to be a good one; she wasn't stupid. Bill spent the next ten minutes calming down his wife and trying to explain that what she saw was not a normal everyday occurrence even though it was. He had always told her that he worked within the safe confines of the Green Zone. This was the only time he had ever lied to his wife. Cunningham had always figured that she would have no way of knowing that he made almost daily trips out to the rest of the city and what she did not know would not hurt her. He had never counted on a news crew following him down the highway with video cameras rolling. They had filmed the entire incident and had it back in time for the evening news. As luck would have it, this was one of the few days Laura had actually turned on the news. They say that timing is everything in life and right now, Bill's timing sucked.

Laura said she had accepted Bill's explanation, but he wasn't buying it. He figured she had come to the conclusion that she would sleep a little better if she just did not know what he actually did. She did not ask anymore and they went back to their usual conversations about where they wanted to go when he came home on leave. Even when he was home, she did not press him to tell her about his job. She was just happy to spend time with him before he went back to the hell hole.

Cunningham had seen a lot of death as a cop. He had even seen other police officers killed in the line of duty. At first he felt sorry for the victims, but over time he became less and less affected by what he saw. Most of death he had to deal with were people who had been killed during the commission of a crime. He still felt compassion for those who had died, but had come to the realization that this was what life was like in the community he worked in. He however, was not ready for what he saw in Iraq.

Death there was not from a single bullet wound. It came in the form of several people or even in extreme cases, hundreds of people being blown to bits by explosions. Death there seemed to be an accepted way of life. Relatives still mourned the dead as anywhere else; they just seemed to be use to it. Cunningham had a hard time coming to grips with this.

One particular incident had Cunningham wondering why he wanted to be there. It happened at an election site during Iraq's first democratic election. Several hundred people where standing in line waiting to vote when a Mercedes sedan approached the group. Seconds later, the car disintegrated in a massive explosion. Hundreds of people were torn to bits by the explosion. The blast was so powerful that the car's engine block was found three blocks away on the roof of a five story building. Cunningham's team happened to come upon the scene about an hour after the explosion. The injured had already been taken away as well as the bodies that could be recovered. A fire truck was hosing the smaller pieces of human body parts as well as all of the blood off the surrounding buildings and roadway. The water carried what remained of the victims into the city's sewer system. While all of this was going on, a hundred or more people had reformed the line waiting to go into the election site. They seemed to act as if nothing had happened. This was something that Cunningham was sure he would never understand.

Bill came to the conclusion that everyone there seemed to hate everyone else who was not part of their particular sect. The two groups in Iraq that are fighting each other are the Sunnis and the Shiites. These are the two main sects within Islam. For the most part, they agree on the fundamental beliefs and practices of Islam. Their abhorrence for one another goes back some fourteen centuries to the death of Muhammad. The divide originated with a dispute over who should succeed the Prophet Muhammad as leader of the Islamic faith he introduced. In other words, they believe in the same thing, but have been fighting each other since 632 A.D. over who ended up being the boss. The one thing that they both agree on is that both groups hate the State of Israel.

CHAPTER 7

Bill's contracted year was finally over and he went home to a grateful wife. She was not only thankful that he had managed to come home safe, but that he had more than provided for her. Cunningham had been well paid and she had managed to put away a great deal of his tax free six hundred and fifty dollar a day salary. Laura couldn't find fault with him when he decided to take a couple of months off to "relax" after coming home. Bill's idea of "relaxing" however was not the same as what his wife had imagined. It was now time to begin bringing all the parts of the plan together.

His first call when he got home was to Jim McGuire. They set up a meeting in Los Angeles and Bill arranged to have Ken fly him to the meeting. Ken had managed to get another flying job. He was transporting planes around the country for a company who sold used airplanes. Ken had to fly a recently sold plane to its new owner in Los Angeles then return to Ft. Lauderdale with the trade in. The trio would spend a couple of days spending some quality time looking over Bill's plan.

Cunningham was going to be careful to only divulge certain parts of the plan to his partners. He did not want the group to know too much of what the others were doing to ensure that no one would accidently slip up. He explained this logic to Jim and Ken and after giving them the general plan, he talked to them individually.

Bill and Jim went to a neighborhood bar around the corner from Jim's house. The bar was dark and not very crowded. They slipped into a booth in the front of the bar. Bill began looking at the black and white pictures which were hung randomly around the bar as the bar maid took their order. They were photos of notable personalities who had stopped into the bar over the years and were all autographed. They appeared to be addressed to some guy named "Rosco" who Bill surmised was the owner. Bill laughed to himself when he noted that the picture directly over Jim's head was of Jimmy Hoffa. He thought to himself, *"How appropriate"*.

Jim noticed Bill checking out the pictures and said "Back in the 50's and 60's this place was a hangout for mobsters and the stars who wanted to be seen with them. The guy who owned it went off to jail and the new owners just left the pictures in place. I guess they liked the ambiance."

Bill lifted his head as if was pointing at the picture behind Jim and said, "Look who you are sitting under".

Jim looked back over his shoulder and let out a little laugh once he figured out who the man with the 50's suit was.

"Ok, what do you need me to do," Jim said after the drinks were placed on the table and the girl who delivered them was walking away.

Bill admired the girl's legs as she was walking away and said "I need you to go to Vegas for a few days and to fix us up with one of your buddies who has a jet".

"Is that all," Jim said with more than a little sarcasm in his voice.

Bill had learned over the years that Jim just worked because he liked to; not because he had to. Jim's family owned huge tracks of land in Mississippi which were covered in Southern Yellow Pine. The building boom in the south during the 80's had made Jim and his family very wealthy. This, combined with the fact that one of his relatives had been the Governor of Mississippi had Jim running in some very impressive circles. Circles in which it was commonplace for the members to have a lot of expensive play toys. Therefore, it wouldn't be too hard for Jim to get one of his friends to let him borrow the family jet.

"The two key elements to this plan are an alibi and the ability to be mobile," Bill responded.

"What's our alibi?" Jim asked.

"You and I are going to be in Vegas when Vince is killed. I'm going to get out of the hotel unnoticed and fly back to Ft. Lauderdale. When I'm done, I fly back and we're covered."

"How are you going to get out of a Vegas hotel unnoticed? Their security cameras have facial identification and can track you anywhere in the hotel."

"I've got that covered with Ken. You'll also use my credit card to buy lunch just to be sure. What about getting a plane?"

"That wouldn't be a problem. I have a friend who rents out his plane when he's not using it," Jim said.

"Good! I want to do this the second or third weekend in October. Find out which date is good for him and we'll go then."

"Anything else?" Jim questioned.

"Can you get an actor or someone who needs some money to play a part and make a couple of phone calls?"

"I should be able to come up with someone. There's a lot of starving actors in this town."

"We need to capitalize on Vince's greed. I want him to think that he's about to make the deal of a lifetime and then he'll do anything to make sure the deal goes through."

Jim took a couple of sips from his glass before asking, "What do you have in mind?"

"Vince's new business is leasing cell phone towers. We need someone to play the part of an owner of a new cell phone company who wants to lease Vince's towers for his new venture. Get me the name of some big time, west coast investor who Vince can check out, but not someone who is real well known. We'll set up an appointment at the last minute and that will make Vince be where I want him at the precise time."

"Actually, I already have someone in mind," Jim said as he called the bar maid over to order two more drinks.

The pair talked about their families until the bar maid returned. Bill once again checked out the girl's legs as she approached the table to deliver their drinks. Jim caught Bill looking and said, "Don't forget you're married" as he took the first sip from his drink.

"You know Laura's Sicilian. There will never be a divorce between us, but a homicide is always a possibility."

"I know what you mean. Listen, Vince isn't stupid. We'll have to act like this is a real business offer. We'll need non-disclosure and other documents to make him believe it's a legitimate deal."

"I think we can get him to do what we want after a couple of phone calls and a non-disclosure. We'll make a call, tell him we want to meet him and send down a non-disclosure for him to sign. FedEx it with the return address of the guy's investment company on it and put their fax number on the paper for him to return it to. Include a note that says the investor is out of town for a day or two so they won't be inclined to call the guy's office. We'll do that a day or two before I hit him, so he doesn't really have time to check it out."

"Sounds like he'll go for it," Jim said after a minute or two of mentally analyzing Bill's plan.

"Pay cash for the FedEx and get a prepaid cell phone which can't be traced. We'll write out a speech for your actor. Monitor the phone call and get the phone back from him when he's done," was Bill's final comment.

The pair finished their drinks and walked back to Jim's house to get Ken. The trio then went off to get some dinner. It was now Ken's turn to hear the part of the plan which involved him. Ken would arrange a ride to Vegas with one of his buddies and then pretend to be Bill while Bill slipped back to South Florida. They were the same size and weight and had matching mustaches. Once again, Bill's police experience came into play. If he left the hotel wearing a baseball cap and a hoodie with the hood over his head, he could then switch clothes with Ken at the airport. Ken could then walk back into the hotel without there being any way to say that it was two different people. Each would just have to walk with their heads down so the security cameras did not get a frontal view of their faces. If they were both careful, it would work.

Ken listened to Bill without saying anything while they ate. He would be able to catch a "jump seat" ride with someone to get to Vegas. All he would have to do is make a few phone calls when the time came to see who was headed west. It was common for pilots to catch rides with friends. It would not be a problem to make sure his ride didn't go into anyone's flight log, so there would be no way to put him in Vegas. He could do the same thing to catch a ride back to Florida. Ken could fly out of Orlando or West Palm Beach which would put him far enough away from Ft. Lauderdale to avoid suspicion. He could then return to the same airport, have Nicky Schapone pick him up and get him back home. If asked, he could say that he caught a ride north with a girl, things didn't work out and he called Nicky to come and pick him up.

The only part of the plan that Ken was unsure of was that Bill wanted him to buy the gun he would use to shoot Vince. Well not the actual rifle, the parts to construct one. Cunningham had a specific list of parts which would allow him to construct a bolt action rifle that took a .308 round. Bill had given Ken a list of gun shows for different cities around the country where the parts could be purchased. As he flew to each city on the list, he was to buy a specific part from a dealer at the show. He purchased the barrel in Albuquerque, the trigger mechanism in Seattle, the stock in Atlanta. Per Bill's instructions, he was only to buy items from the dealer's personal stock and to pay cash. He had given Ken different manufacturers to choose from for the items he needed, but was very specific on which scope he wanted; a Leupold VX3.

Once Bill and Ken returned home, Bill called Jay to meet him for lunch. Bill's instructions for Jay were simple. He was to change his schedule. Jay was to work for the police department on a couple of days during the week in September instead of the weekends, so his request to work on the day it happened would not seem out of place. He was also to request an assignment to Zone 3, the police zone which covered South Pine Island Road. Jay's assignment would then be to work the crime scene as normal, with the exception of covertly looking over the area where Cunningham had positioned himself to make sure nothing that could be used as evidence was left behind. If asked, he was to tell the detectives who would be on the case anything they wanted to know about anyone's past connection with Vince.

Chapter 8

Bill and his passenger sat in a pickup which was parked in Ken Martin's driveway. It was 4 a.m. and the sun would not be up for a couple of hours, but Bill was a little more comfortable doing what he now had to do while it was still dark. The plan was ready to be set in motion in a few days, but there was one important detail that had to wait until now to be completed. Bill looked over at his passenger.

"You alright?" Bill asked.

"Yes, I think so."

"You'll do fine. Just listen to what these guys tell you to do and you'll be alright."

"How do you know them?"

"I met them while I was working narcotics, but don't worry, I trust them to do what they have been hired for. They will get you there without any problems and they won't ask questions. These guys make their living doing this and they wouldn't stay in business long if they couldn't be trusted," Bill said.

"Let's go over this one more time just to make sure."

"No problem. The boat will take you over to the Bahamas and stop a few miles offshore from Freeport. They will then have another small boat come out and pick you up and take you to a private cove on the island. A car will be waiting there to take you to the airport."

"I'm not going to have a problem at the airport am I?"

"No. The customs official will have been paid a couple of hundred bucks and he'll look the other way. They put a stamp in your passport and no one is the wiser on how you got to the Bahamas. The driver will have your airline ticket to get you to the airport in time for your flight," Bill said.

"It sounds too simple."

"It really is if you hire the right people. Did you clear everything with Vince?"

"I told him I was going up to Orlando for a couple of days and he was okay with it. He doesn't know what I do half of the time anyways."

Their conversation was interrupted when Bill heard the deep rumble of exhaust from the boat which was now docking behind Ken's house. Bill handed his passenger the list of the three banks in the Cayman Islands where the bank accounts needed to be set up. The two then exited Bill's truck and walked around to the rear of Ken's home. There, waiting for them was a sleek, all white forty five foot speed boat; known in the boating community as a "Go Fast" boat.

Bill waved at the man standing at the boat's controls as the pair walked up to the dock. The passenger became a little apprehensive when they saw how young the "man" actually was. He was no older than twenty or twenty two at the most.

"You sure about this?" the passenger whispered to Bill as they stepped up on the dock. Bill, seeing that his passenger was now questioning the wisdom of this part of his plan said, "He has been doing this for at least six years that I know of and hasn't been caught yet."

"It's the "caught yet" part that bothers me."

"Stop worrying. The worst that will happen is that you will get a fine for entering the Bahamas illegally. If that happens, I'll make some adjustments to the plan, but it won't make any difference in the long run. Everything is going to be put in motion in a day or two and we can work around this part if we need to."

The passenger was then helped onto the boat and took a seat at the stern of the boat. Bill helped untie the lines and pushed the front of the boat away from the dock. He gave a wave to the boat's captain and his passenger as he turned to go back to his truck.

Chapter 9

Barbara had taken the job at the restaurant to help pay the bills. She was recently divorced and was receiving alimony, but it was not quite enough to raise her two kids properly. Even before her divorce was final, she had been checking Jay out when he came in to eat. Her marriage had been in trouble for a long time and if he had asked, she would have gone out with him. She found it odd that Jay was in on a Thursday and not his usual weekend shift, but she was still happy that he had sat in her section.

"What are you doing here? Get fired from your regular job?" Barbara said trying to start up a conversation. Jay found himself totally distracted because the day they had all waited for had finally arrived. It did not immediately register with him that she had asked him a question. She waited and when he didn't respond, she turned to walk away. He seemed to be lost in thought, but finally turned and said, "Sorry, I didn't catch that."

"Oh, nothing. I was just wondering what you were doing here on a Thursday."

"Just needed a break from my other job."

Barbara knew that Jay worked as a reserve officer because he liked police work and that he was some type of supervisor at a hospital in another county. She wasn't sure what he did, but assumed it was very stressful. "Anything I can do for you," Barbara said and realized after she said it that her statement had come across as rather suggestive.

"No. Not now. I've got a lot on my mind. Can I just get some coffee?"

Barbara, who was now a little embarrassed, turned and left to go pour Jay his coffee. Before she was able to return, Jay's police radio came to life and his adrenaline began pumping when he heard the alert tone. "Charlie 3 and any units in the area. Signal 4 with injuries; South Pine Island Road at Gatehouse Road. Charlie 3, handle code three." Jay was already moving for the door when he heard the alert tone. Barbara turned, almost dropping Jay's cup of coffee and yelled out something Jay couldn't make out. He jumped into his police car and pushed the buttons that would turn on his vehicle's overhead lights and siren. He hit the accelerator hard and spun the police unit's tires as he exited the restaurant's parking lot.

Jay had been expecting the emergency call he was now responding to. That is why he had been preoccupied in the restaurant, but a traffic accident? Maybe something went wrong. Maybe Bill could not take the shot because someone else had gotten into an accident at the same intersection; or worse, maybe his shot caused the accident.

Jay approached from the north and saw a vehicle on the southeast corner of the intersection as he pulled up. The car had hit a light pole and was smoking badly. There were two other cars stopped in the northbound lanes just short of the accident. Jay drove across all of the southbound lanes and parked his car diagonally across the northbound lanes to protect the scene. He jumped out of his car and ran over to what he now saw was a Mercedes Benz. Goldman was unsure of what he would find when he got to the car, because he realized Bill had never told him what Vince would be driving that day.

Jay reached the driver's door and saw a male slumped over in the driver's seat with his head on the steering wheel. Jay tried to open the driver's door, but found that it had been buckled by the accident. He then ran around to the passenger's door, only to find it locked. As he did so, he keyed the microphone of his radio and asked for backup units for traffic control and the fire department for a trapped victim. Goldman pulled out a punch tool from a pouch on his gun belt. He carried it for just this type of emergency and struck the glass as hard as he could with the tool. The impact caused the glass to shatter and he reached in to open the door. He leaned in and first turned the key to kill the engine. Goldman then examined the unconscious man to see where he was injured.

Jay saw that the man was bleeding from wounds in both the front and back of his neck. He glanced at the windshield and noticed several cracks in it from the accident. He also saw what may have been a small hole just above the dash board. He looked again at the man, but was still unsure if this was Vince. The man was much older looking and heavier than Jay imagined Vince would be. Before he could investigate the man's identify any further, a paramedic was pulling at his arm, so that he could take Jay's place in the car. Jay was not surprised by their quick response. The rescue units would have been dispatched at the same time he was for this type of accident. As Jay backed out of the car he noticed that a fire truck had also arrived and that the firemen were bringing out the "Jaws of Life" in order to pry open the driver's door.

Jay backed away and examined the scene. As far as he could see, there were no other vehicles involved in the accident. There were two other vehicles that had parked alongside the road which contained witnesses to the accident. The only other vehicles at the scene were a couple of "rubberneckers" who were passing by and were more interested in the accident than where they were going. Jay turned his attention to directing what little traffic there was around the accident scene.

Two other police units had now arrived, so Jay turned his attention from traffic control to the witnesses. Goldman pulled out his notepad and wrote down their names and what they had seen. Both drivers told pretty much the same story. They were traveling north and began slowing down when the traffic light at the intersection had changed from green to yellow. They were both startled when the Mercedes, which had been stopped on the west side of the intersection, suddenly raced across the street and struck the light pole for no apparent reason. One of the drivers surmised that the driver must have had a heart attack; the other thought he was drunk. It was about this time that one of the other cops walked over to Jay.

"Here's the guy's wallet. You had better go over and talk to the medics; this isn't an accident. The guy's got a bullet hole in his neck."

"A what!" Jay said in a somewhat surprised voice. His reaction was not an act. He was truly shocked that the driver had been shot.

"A bullet hole! Looks like someone shot the guy. I guess while he was stopped over there," the other officer said as he pointed to where the witnesses had said the car had been waiting on the light. Jay opened the wallet and found the man's Florida driver's license; the name Vincent Maganelli was printed on the license which had a picture that Jay noticed did not look at all like the Vince he had known. He then walked back over to the car. As he did so, Jay scanned the surrounding area and the parking lot of the medical building that was just across the street from the accident. He was not sure what he was looking for. He just knew what he didn't want to see; Bill Cunningham.

Jay walked up to Jerry Orland, a seasoned paramedic who was standing by the car and watching the others tend to the victim.

"Hey Jay. What a way to start a morning. You had better call out the detectives. This wasn't an accident. It looks like it's going to be a homicide."

"Is Vince dead?" Jay said and immediately realized that he had given away knowing the victim. If Jerry had found Jay's familiarity with the victim unusual, he didn't let on as he said, "No, but he's going to be. We're having trouble controlling the bleeding and people just don't survive getting hit where this guy got shot." Jay stepped back and watched as the medics worked on Vince. He keyed his mike and asked the dispatcher to contact detectives to have them respond to what was now a possible homicide. As he waited for the detectives to arrive, Jay scanned the area one more time to make sure there was no sign of Cunningham.

Detective Robert Cappiello looked over the scene before exiting his car. His partner, Detective Steve Miller had already exited their car and was talking to Goldman at the rear of the Mercedes. Robert or Robbie as he was known around the station liked to observe and left Miller to ask the questions. He found that he could read a person's body language and hear nuances in their voices which helped him determine if they were being truthful. Robbie did his best work when he was not doing the talking. Miller was walking back to their car when Robbie finally got out.

"You're not going to believe this. Goldman went to Plantation High with the victim. Looks like he took a round through the throat. Medics said it will be a miracle if he makes it."

"We got witnesses," Robbie asked while looking at where the Mercedes had ended up.

"Yeah, they said that the Mercedes was stopped over there on Gatehouse and that he just shot across the intersection and struck the pole. They didn't hear any gun shots and there were no other cars around."

Robbie didn't respond as he watched the victim get loaded into the ambulance. A few seconds later it was on its way to the hospital. He looked back at Miller and said, "Get over to the hospital in case this guy comes to and I'll hang around for forensics." As Miller drove off, Robbie went and stood in the middle of the intersection. He began developing a mental picture as to how this had all unfolded. He had looked at the bullet hole in the windshield and its exit hole through the back window. Robbie also talked to the witnesses before he let them go, so he knew exactly where the Mercedes had been stopped. He then walked over to the northeast corner of the intersection. *"The ornamental grasses over there would make a good hiding place,"* he thought to himself. He continued to examine the area, periodically looking across to the other side of the intersection.

Goldman had been watching Detective Cappiello and walked over, trying not to have any expression that might give away the fact that he had information about the case that he did not want to share. Robbie had begun to walk around the grassy area and Jay followed. Jay saw what he thought was a depressed area in the middle of the grass, indicating that someone had laid there. He dare not show too much interest in the area just in case Robbie had missed it. He wanted to take a closer look to check the area as Cunningham had instructed, but stayed next to Robbie and viewed the area from a distance.

"Jay, you the first one on the scene?" Robbie finally asked.

"Yeah, came in as a signal four with injuries."

"Miller said you knew the guy."

"Since high school. He moved away for a while, but moved back a few years ago."

"You keep in touch?" Robbie asked as he began to walk towards where the Mercedes had stopped. Jay followed and said, "No, haven't talked to him since high school. I know he had a business here, but I never contacted him." By then, Robbie had reached the middle of the intersection and looked back at the corner. He then focused on the building which was located beyond the parking lot. While he was doing this, a white police van pulled up to the scene and two crime scene technicians exited. After getting their equipment out of the back of the van, they began talking to the first patrolman they saw. Robbie turned to Jay and said, "Have the forensic people go over to the medical building and pull their surveillance tape. I want to see what's on it." Jay turned and walked towards the technicians as Robbie once again looked over the intersection; looking for anything he might have missed.

After forming a clear mental picture of the scene and how he believed this incident had unfolded, Detective Cappiello caught a ride back to the station with a patrolman and sat down at his desk. He was waiting for Miller to return from the hospital. As he did, he looked at the dozen or so manila folders covering his desk. Each one represented an open case which would now have to go on the back burner. A homicide, particularly one that appeared to be an assassination would be front page news and everyone from the chief of police to the mayor, not to mention the media would want answers which he did not have.

Robert Salvatore Cappiello had been a cop in Plantation since the mid-seventies. He never really had a choice about becoming a police officer. Both of his brothers, his father, an uncle and his grandfather were all cops in New York City. The only difference between him and them was that he hated the cold. NYPD was not the place he wanted to be a cop. After graduating from NYU, he applied to police departments all over the south and had to listen to his family's objections about his breaking the family tradition.

Cappiello joined the Plantation Police Department over everyone's objections and had worked his way up from patrol officer to detective. He moved throughout the detective division, working every type of case there was and finally landed in the Homicide Division. That had been ten years and about a hundred pounds ago. His Italian heritage had left him a little short in stature, so the extra weight was noticeable. He had thick hands, a thick neck and a thick waistline. Robbie had wanted to lose the weight, but his case load didn't allow him any gym time; at least that's what he told himself when he looked in the mirror each morning. For the most part, his kids had grown up without a father due to his job and over the past year his wife had been after him to retire so they could finally spend some time together. He loved his job, but he was becoming tired of the daily grind. As he looked at his desk and then at the stack of unsolved cases; he decided then and there that this was going to be his last case.

CHAPTER 10

Cunningham had immediately left the area and headed east. He was on this way to get rid of the rifle which would identity him as the shooter. As he approached his destination, he glanced over at the Compsale sign as he drove down Griffin Road. He pulled the Chevy van into the parking lot of a small warehouse complex which ironically was just down the road from Vince's office. Bill pulled around to the back of one of the warehouse bays and carefully looked around to see if anyone else was there. When he was sure that he was alone, he unlocked the overhead door of one of the bays and opened it. He quickly pulled the van into the warehouse and closed the door behind him.

The warehouse belonged to Nicky Schapone, who used it to earn some extra money machining parts for different customers. Nicky had a small machine shop with a Bridgeport vertical mill, a lathe and other miscellaneous machines that he could use to earn some extra money by producing custom parts for businesses in the area. Bill looked around and spotted what he was looking for. Nicky had not only purchased the Chevy van, but had bought an extra driver's front door, a rear door and bumper for it. They were a different color than the van's and showed a lot of wear and tear. Bill had gotten to work removing the van's front bumper when the front door opened and Nicky walked in.

"I heard it on the news coming over here," Nicky said.

"I know. Can we just get to work? I don't want to talk about it right now."

Nicky saw that Bill was visibly upset, so he quietly walked over to the van and began loosening the passenger side bumper bolts as

Bill worked on the other side. The two worked in silence and finished exchanging the parts Nicky had purchased. Bill stopped and began wiping the grease and dirt from his hands with a shop rag. He looked over at Nicky who was now doing the same thing and decided he needed to say something.

"I couldn't look at Vince after I pulled the trigger. I just saw his car go across the intersection. I was unsure how I would feel right now, but I don't really feel anything. I don't regret that I did it, but I'm not happy that I shot him either. I just don't know how I feel right now."

"Did anyone see you leave?"

"Everyone was too busy with Vince and I was out of there before the first unit pulled up. I drove over here nice and slow so no one would notice me. I think we're ok."

"We all agreed that you needed to do this, and we're all in this together. Let's just finish what we need to do and move on," Nicky said trying to reassure Bill that he had done the right thing.

"I'll finish up on the van if you can take care of the rifle," Bill said.

Nicky opened the back door of the van and removed the rifle. He put it on a work bench and began dismantling the weapon. After removing the scope and barrel, he reached under the work bench and pulled out a plastic bag which contained a matching rifle barrel. Since all the parts of the rifle had been bought separately, there would be no record that would show which serial numbers were on the finished weapon. Bill had wanted to keep the rifle just in case anyone was able to link the parts to Ken and then to him. By changing the barrel, he eliminated the chance that a ballistics test on the bullet would ever be matched to that rifle. He also changed out the firing pin so the markings on the bullet casing would be different even though Bill had been careful to remove the spent casing from the rifle and disposed of it in a canal as he passed by. Nicky placed the used barrel in a vice and began cutting it into small pieces which then could be disposed of. When he finished with the barrel he took a file to the old firing pin. When that was done, Nicky grabbed a garbage bag and stuffed the ghillie suit into it. He would burn it in his back yard barbeque pit later on.

Nicky had been the first one Bill had talked to about his plan. Nicky and Dave were best friends ever since they had met in the fifth grade. Nicky was working as a master machinist at a company making tool and die parts used to produce jet engine parts for the military when Bill and Dave hired him to work at Cunningham. Nicky would have to take a huge pay cut to go to work as a machinist for the brothers, but he didn't mind. He was glad to help his friends get their business off the ground and knew that when the business took off he would be rewarded for his efforts. When Bill and Dave were forced out, Vince fired Nicky. He didn't want them to have a sympathetic friend still working at the business who could feed them information. After leaving Cunningham's, Nicky was rehired by his old company, but at a greatly reduced salary. This gave Schapone even more incentive to make everything right.

Bill continued to work on the van. He finished bolting on the doors then sprayed primer paint to one of the fenders. He wanted to make sure that the van no longer looked like the one which would eventually be seen in the security video. When the barrel was done, Nicky came over to help Bill finish up. It was now time to work on the engine. Bill changed the engine timing slightly and took off one the engine's valve covers. He loosened several of the bolts holding the intake values in place. This would cause the engine to run roughly and there would be a knocking sound, giving the impression that the engine was about to give out.

They had just one more thing to do. Remove any trace Bill had ever been in the vehicle. Cunningham began systematically vacuuming out the vehicle, making sure not miss a single inch of the interior while Nicky wiped the entire vehicle down with a rag. When they finished, Nicky picked up the rifle from the work bench and wrapped it in an old towel he had in the shop. He then went out to put it in the trunk of his car. Bill pulled the van out of the bay and after locking up, drove around to the front of the building to meet up with Nicky.

"You already talk to the junk yard?" Bill asked.

"Yeah, they said to bring it over this morning and they would take it in. I told them exactly what you said. The engine is gone and it will cost too much to replace, so I just want to sell it for parts."

Nicky entered the van and drove it out of the warehouse parking lot towards State Route 7 where the salvage yard was located. Bill followed in Nicky's car and parked at the far end of the salvage yard's parking lot where no one would see him. Bill saw Nicky and one of the guys from the yard comparing the information on the van's title to the vehicle identification number on the van. They went back inside the business, finished the paperwork and Nicky emerged a short time later.

"Everything go ok?" Bill asked.

"Yeah, they gave me two hundred and fifty dollars for a van that cost us a thousand. Remind me never to go into business with you again." Nicky said trying to relieve some of the pressure of the situation. Bill jumped over into the passenger's seat and Nicky started driving north towards Interstate 595. Nicky followed the interstate to Interstate 95, and then turned northbound. Neither of them said much on the drive, preferring to listen to the oldies station on the car's radio. After driving for about forty minutes, they exited the interstate at Glades Road and headed towards the Boca Raton Airport. Nicky pulled up to the front of a private hanger and watched as Bill got out of the car.

Bill reached back in and shook Nicky's hand. He couldn't find anything to say. Nicky had agreed that this needed to be done. He had been helping Bill right from the start; more so than any of the others. He trusted Nicky more than the others in the group. They were the closest and that's why he had Nicky help him fine tune certain aspects of the plan.

During the planning stage, Cunningham told Nicky about how he had met Miguel, a sniper instructor from Silverback Independent in Canyon, Texas. Bill had met him at the airport in Amman, Jordan during one of his R&R trips from Iraq and this chance meeting was an unexpected plus in Bill's planning.

He was sitting in the bar at the La Mirage Amman Hotel and Miguel was the only other American in the place. They had a few beers and compared where they had worked in Iraq. The conversation eventually turned to guns and ammunition and how shitty it was to work in Iraq. Bill saw an opening and asked about shooting at car windshields; something that PSD's did quite a lot on the streets of Baghdad. Miguel told him that a windshield would deflect a bullet traveling through it. Something that Cunningham had witnessed firsthand as a cop. He remembered the day when several officers had fired bullets through a car's windshield at a robbery suspect and not one found its intended target. Cunningham realized that he would have to do some target practice if he was going to place the shot where he wanted it. There was a problem however, he couldn't just go out and borrow someone's Mercedes to take a few shots at.

The solution was simple; build a Mercedes replica for his target. This is where Nicky's experience came in. He helped Bill drive to an auto salvage yard in Atlanta to purchase four windshields from damaged Mercedes SL 550 Roadsters. They had found a salvage yard that did not mind cash and more importantly, didn't ask questions. They then painstakingly built a framework and mounted a windshield into it which was at the correct height and angle of his target vehicle. Bill practiced on his replica until he was able to find the correct aiming point which would allow him to pin point his shot.

Bill was also relying on Nicky's machine shop expertise to build him a silencer. He would be concealed, but the sound of a rifle shot would instantly give his position away. Cunningham had found *Hog-Shot*, an internet forum used mostly by Marine snipers to exchange information. From his time in Iraq, he had learned that a Marine who was going through sniper school was referred to as a "Pig". When they completed their training they were awarded a hog's tooth and became known as "Hogs". Bill figured a forum which called itself *Hog-Shot* had to be a good place to get the additional information he needed.

Cunningham had done some research on the site and was able to come up with a picture of a silencer. He gave it to Nicky who was able to build an exact replica. An impressive feat considering he only had a picture to work from. They had tested out the silencer at an old, abandoned orange grove near Sebring, Florida. Once they knew the silencer worked and the rifle had the proper aiming point on the windshield without deflecting the bullet, they cut up the frame and disposed of all its components in the canals along their route home.

Bill was still unable to find just the right thing to say to Nicky, so he closed the door and headed for the hanger. Nicky immediately rolled down the passenger door window and called out to Bill, "I almost forgot to give this to you." Bill stopped and walked back to the car. Nicky reached over and handed Bill a small brown paper bag through the open window. Bill looked at it with a smile and placed it in his jacket pocket saying, "This is important. I'm glad you didn't forget it."

The jet which had brought him to Boca Raton from Las Vegas was standing by to make the return trip. McGuire had arranged for the use of the plane from a friend of his and was assured that the pilots would be discrete if asked about their cargo. Jim and his friend had made a deal with a local wine shop in Boca to import a special wine from Chile; thirty cases worth to be exact. He had sent the plane to make the pickup and if there were undocumented passengers catching a ride on the plane, it was ok with the plane's owner. Bill saw Nicky pull out of the parking lot just as he boarded the plane for his return trip. Jim and Ken would be meeting him at Henderson Executive Airport in Vegas. The plane's owner had a private hanger which would allow Bill and Ken to switch places out of view of anyone's prying eyes. Ken would then return back to Florida, but he would fly into Orlando where Nicky was now headed to pick him up later in the day. This way the detectives could make all the inquiries they wanted at the local airports, but would come up empty handed.

CHAPTER 11

Detective Cappiello was right about the attention the shooting would get. His captain relayed a message from the mayor that he wanted this case solved as quickly as possible. "The mayor doesn't want any more "Mafia hits" in his town," was how the Captain had put it. They were already reporting the "gangland" style shooting on the local news at noon. Miller had called him from the hospital saying that Maganelli was in surgery, but that the doctor did not hold out much hope that the surgery would be successful. He had also talked to the forensic team who said they had virtually nothing to go on. All they had were some pictures of the scene and a surveillance video, but that was about it. They were unable to locate the bullet or determine exactly where the shooter had been, but thought he had been in the planted ornamental bed on the northeast corner of the intersection. In other words, they had nothing which would make Cappiello's last case an easy one. He told everyone to be in the office at 2 pm.

Robbie sat at the head of the conference table in the detective squad room and looked at his "team" who were sitting around the table. The captain had assigned two more detectives to him to help out; Sam Bonner and Tom Schultz. Both had been detectives for about five years and would be handling the leg work. Miller would work with Robbie and handle the more sensitive matters. The forensic technicians would do their own thing, but Robbie wanted a direct line of communication so he could act quickly on anything they found. Cappiello's captain and the department's Public Information Officer were also present and standing in the corner of the room. He would let the captain and the

PIO handle the media. A job they both relished, but one Robbie made it a point to avoid. Robbie laid out how he wanted the investigation conducted and what each person's responsibility would be. He got everyone's attention by saying, "We either have a random nut running around out there or this was a professional hit. We need to find out which it is and fast. The first order of business we need to do is talk to the family, friends and business associates of our victim." He then told each member of the team what they would be responsible for.

As the meeting broke up, Robbie pulled Bonner aside and told him to go and talk to Patrolman Goldman. "I talked to him out at the scene and I think there's something that he's not telling me," Cappiello said. Schultz and Bonner headed off to track down Jay and to begin a records search to see what they could learn about the victim. Robbie and Miller went to their car and drove out of the station to go and talk with Maganelli's wife; Christine. She was at home and not at the hospital which Robbie found odd, but he had learned a long time ago that people who were anticipating the loss of a loved one sometimes acted strangely and not as one would expect.

The detectives were stopped by the guard in the security booth at the end of Gatehouse Road who began questioning them as to why they were there. Miller, trying not to get too pissed off showed the guard his detective badge and said, "We're going to the Maganelli home on Coco Plum Circle." The guard, thinking twice about questioning the detectives any further, raised the drop arm and let them go through.

"Maganelli must have done well for himself," Miller said as they parked the unmarked unit in the driveway of the Maganelli home. "This thing has to be a million easy," Robbie replied. The house was typical of big money homes in South Florida. They had parked on a stamped concrete driveway which was laid out in a herringbone pattern. The driveway led up to a two story peach colored home which had a Spanish style roof and expensive landscaping surrounding the entire house. The two were welcomed at the front door by the family's maid and led into a den, just off the living room where they were asked to wait for "Señora Maganelli". Christine Maganelli joined them in the den after a few minutes later.

Robbie introduced himself and Detective Miller. He then went through his routine speech about how sorry they were and that they hated to intrude during her hour of need, but they needed to get some information from her. A speech he hated to do, but one that he had done so many times before it just flowed from his mouth without him actually thinking about it. Robbie watched Mrs. Maganelli's body language as she explained how she just couldn't bear to be at the hospital and watch her husband's life come to an end. The detectives asked the standard questions and got the routine answers they expected; Vince Maganelli had no enemies and she couldn't think of anyone who wanted to harm him. Mrs. Maganelli did reveal however, that her husband had left the house earlier than normal. He always left at 9 am. As a matter of fact, he was religious about leaving the house at 9, but for some reason he had left early today.

The detectives assured her that they would do everything in their power to solve the crime and had Mrs. Maganelli promise to contact them if she thought of anything that could help their investigation. They left their business cards with Mrs. Maganelli and were shown to the door. As they stopped by their car, Robbie looked at Miller and said, "Did you find her reaction to our questions a little strange? Like she knew something she didn't want to tell us."

"I took it as her being nervous and being under a lot of stress. She's sitting there waiting to hear that her husband didn't make it through surgery."

"I'm not sure about that. I'm reading something else there. We need to find out how this guy made his money," Robbie said as the two entered their car and drove back to the station. Sandy, one of the forensic technicians was waiting for the pair and met Robbie at the back door of the police station.

"You wanted me to tell you if we had anything new on that shooting," Sandy said to Robbie.

"You have something good?"

"A lady from the apartments there on Gatehouse called in. She found what she thinks is a bullet hole in her door. I'm on my way over there now."

"Let me know as soon as you have something. I want to know what type of weapon we're dealing with," Robbie said as Sandy began walking away.

"As soon as I know, you'll know," Sandy called back over her shoulder as she made her way to her vehicle.

The next morning, Cappiello was in the office well before any of his team showed up. He had received the photographs of the scene from Sandy and had pinned them up on his bulletin board. He was standing, studying the picture of the bullet hole in the Mercedes' windshield when Miller came in.

"I saw Sandy last night when she came back from that apartment on Gatehouse," Steve said.

"What did she say," Robbie asked without looking away from the pictures.

"She said it was a three-o-eight, but that she had never seen anything like it. The round didn't fragment or even change shape for that matter. She has the whole bullet; it's in good shape and should be able to match it if we can find the gun."

Robbie finally looked away from the pictures and said, "I guess that eliminates the nut case theory since they generally don't arm themselves with exotic rounds. We had better check out this guy's past and his businesses to see who doesn't like him very much."

"I'm way ahead of you. Maganelli owns a business called Compsale and I talked to his business manager. He'll see us this morning. I was also able to get some basic information about his businesses off the computer."

The detectives found Compsale in the same location where the Cunningham's had first talked to Vince about their idea. They entered the business and asked to speak to John LaBrock, Vince's business manager. They were escorted into a corner office where they found LaBrock sitting behind his desk.

As Robbie entered the office he examined Labrock sitting behind a large mahogany desk and noted that Labrock was of Latin or Italian decent. He appeared to be a little shorter than average and thin. He was dressed in a very expensive imported suit and sported a gold watch which Robbie guessed would have cost more than the car he was driving on a cop's salary.

"Hi, I'm John LaBrock. Thank you for coming by so quickly. I want to help you get whoever did this to Vince, so ask me anything," John said as he pointed for the detectives to sit down in chairs which were in front of his desk. Robbie smiled a little when he realized that LaBrock's voice and mannerisms reminded him of the "Riddler" from the *Batman* television show.

"We're hoping you can fill us in on Mr. Maganelli's business interests. We have little to go on at this time and it would be a help to fully understand what he was involved in," Robbie asked.

"I've been Vince's business manager for about eleven years now and know everything he had going on."

"We see that Mr. Maganelli has been involved in several businesses over the years. The State shows that he is listed as an officer in at least three different companies since 1992," Miller said.

"Yes, that's correct. He started Compsale in 1992, started a company called Cunningham Fuel Injection in '96 and Towercell in 2002. That's a cell phone tower leasing company."

"We first need to know if Mr. Maganelli had any enemies or if he recently received any threats," Robbie asked.

"No, nothing like that. Vince has made a lot of money over the years and I guess he could have stepped on some people's toes. He did have a problem with his business partners from Cunningham, but they settled the case in court and Vince paid them off."

"Do you know where he was going yesterday morning? His wife said that it left the house earlier than normal."

"Yes. He was going to meet with an investor who was going to lease our cell phone towers for a new phone company which was starting up."

"Were you going to meet him also?" Miller asked as he wrote down what he heard in his notebook.

"No. I set up the meeting, but Vince said he wanted to meet the guy by himself to feel him out. The investor, a guy named Marshall Kent from LaPointe, Brewster and Smith in California called us; we checked out him and his company. He sounded legit so I set up the meeting."

"You mention that he had a legal battle with some other partners. Did that end peacefully?" Robbie asked.

"I would say so. Vince is an aggressive businessman and his methods are not always appreciated, especially if you're on the receiving end. These two brothers, Dave and Bill Cunningham came up with an idea for a fuel injection system which could be sold in the aftermarket. Vince was originally from New York, but lived here when he was younger and knew these guys from high school, so he backed their idea. Things weren't going well, so he took over the business and forced the brothers out. They weren't happy, so they sued. The suit was settled out of court."

"You said they went to school together. Would that be Plantation High School?" Robbie asked as he glanced over to see if Steve had picked up on the comment.

"Yeah, Vince lived here while he was in high school, moved away for a while, but moved back in '91, I think it was."

Robbie asked a few more questions and obtained what information LaBrock had on Vince's past business partners and the information on Kent. The two detectives left the meeting with more questions than answers. Cappiello asked Miller to get the court documents on the Cunningham's law suit and to contact LaPointe and company to find out about the meeting with Maganelli. Miller sat in the passenger seat, reviewing the notes he took. "I get the feeling that there was a whole lot more information we didn't get out of LaBrock," Miller said. Robbie looked over at his partner and said, "You're learning. That guy didn't tell us everything he knows."

Miller made some phone calls once the pair returned to the station. He sent Bonner and Schultz to the Broward County Courthouse to get a copy of the lawsuit involving the Cunningham's. He made all of the necessary arrangements to get Maganelli's phone records along with those of Compsale, Towercell and LaBrock. He also decided that he needed to talk to Goldman one more time. Steve placed the call to St Mary's hospital where Jay was on duty.

"Jay, its Steve Miller."

"What can I do for you," Jay said.

"Do you know two brothers named Cunningham?"

"Yes I do. They went to school with Vince and I. We've all known each other since the fifth grade. Why?"

"Their names came up as knowing Maganelli."

Jay remembered everything Bill had told him and was going to give Steve complete answers to the questions he asked. "Yeah, they had a business with Vince a few years back. Vince screwed them out of the business and they had to sue him. They settled and made a few bucks out of the deal."

"Why didn't you tell me this at the scene?"

"For starters, I didn't think of it. I was a little busy at the time. I didn't get along with Vince, so that's why I didn't keep up with him when he moved back to Florida. Bill and Dave are friends of mine, but we never talked about Vince when we talked about their business because they knew I didn't like him. They got a good settlement and moved on."

"What do they do now?"

"Dave's dead. He died of cancer a couple of years ago and Bill just got back from Iraq in July."

"Iraq! What did he do there?"

Jay followed Bill's instructions and didn't leave anything out.

"Bill had been a Ft. Lauderdale cop for several years before he left to start up the business with Vince. When that didn't work out, a company hired him because of his tactical training to go and work in Baghdad. He was a PSD, but I'm not real sure what he did."

"Ok, thanks. If I need anything else I'll get in touch with you."

Miller hung up the phone and looked over at Robbie who occupied the desk directly across from his.

"You're not going to believe this one. Bill Cunningham was a cop for Ft Lauderdale PD and he went off to Iraq to be a mercenary. He just got back a couple of months ago."

Robbie looked up from a paper he was reviewing and said, "We need to start looking at that guy and see where he was on Thursday."

About that time, Sandy walked in to the detective's office holding a VCR tape over head and saying, "Look what I've got." The three went into an interrogation room where there was a TV with a video player and plugged in the tape. Sandy fast forwarded the tape to a section she wanted the detectives to see.

"There's a white Chevy van which pulls into the parking lot at zero five forty two and drives to the back corner of the parking lot, but no one gets out," Sandy said as she fast forwarded the tape to the time the accident happened.

"The dispatch time on the call was zero seven-o-four. The van pulls out at zero seven-o-six. There is nothing else on the tape except the victim's car crashing into the light pole," Sandy said.

"We got anything on the white van? Robbie asked.

"No. The van was backed in and there was nothing on the front," Sandy said referring to the fact that Florida doesn't have license tags on the front of its vehicles.

"The van sits there the entire time and no one gets out? Let's rerun that part again." Robbie said. Sandy backed the tape up and replayed that section.

"I've watched the whole tape twice now and no one gets out. You can see both ..."

Robbie interrupted Sandy, pointed at the television screen and said, "What's that?" He was pointing to a clump of grass that suddenly seemed to appear in the ornamental bed located just behind the parked van. "Back that up. I want to see that again," Robbie said. Sandy reran the tape.

"That's our shooter. He's right there in that clump of grass where I thought he would be," Robbie stated.

"How did he get there? No one gets out of the van and you can see all sides of that bed," Miller questioned.

"You can't really see the back doors in the tape. The van is positioned so the camera doesn't pick up the rear doors," Robbie explained.

"We're talking a pro then; someone really checked this area out," Miller pointed out.

"Well maybe not a professional. Maybe it's someone who just thinks like a pro; like a cop. Let's find out where Cunningham is and go talk to him," Robbie said.

CHAPTER 12

Cappiello had barely been home for two days. He had only been there long enough to take a shower and get a little sleep. Even though it was early Saturday morning, he was already preparing to go back into work.

"Please don't tell me you're going in today," Sally asked in a somewhat disgusted voice. She had been through this too many times before. Sally had been Robbie's wife for thirty years. She met him while he was still in the police academy and fell in love with both the man and the uniform. Over the years, she had put up with all of the issues of being married to a policeman. The midnight shifts, the overtime and the not knowing if she was ever going to see him again when he left the house for work, but her patience was wearing thin.

"The case will wait until Monday. We have plans to go to the mall and we're having dinner at my brother's house tonight; remember?" she said while barely holding her temper.

Robbie knew that there was now going to be a fight that he just didn't want to have. "I can't. This case is just too important. I've got the Mayor wanting this thing solved now."

"I'm tired of you putting work before this family. Every time they call, you go. You're the senior detective. Why can't Miller or Bonner take the lead for once?"

"This is just too important."

"Robbie, you think all of your cases are important. What's important is your family."

"I can't deal with this right now. I sorry about the shopping, but I promise I'll be home in time to go to your brothers," Robbie said as he headed out the front door.

Robbie knew Sally was right. He stopped half way out of the driveway and went back into the house. He found Sally sitting in the kitchen pretending to look at the morning's paper. She didn't even look up when he walked in.

"Listen, I know you're right. I made up my mind that this is my last case. I was going to tell the captain on Monday morning to start my paperwork. You have to understand that this case is important. Not only because it might turn into a homicide, but because it's my last case. I want to go out with a conviction, but I don't have anything strong to go on right now. I need to make sure that whoever did this doesn't get away. Not just to put someone behind bars, but for me. Knowing I went out on a positive note."

"Robbie! You don't have to prove you're a good detective to me or anyone you work with. I know it and so do they." Sally was silent for a moment then continued. "If it's that important to you, then I guess I can put up with it for a little while longer, but I'm holding you to it; this is the last one."

Robbie bent over and gave his wife a kiss and headed back out to his car. As he did so, he called Miller to make sure he was on the way in. He also told Miller to make sure Bonner and Schultz were there.

Miller arrived at the detective bureau with four cups of coffee and a dozen donuts. He didn't like the stereo type image of cops and donuts, but it was Saturday morning after all and he wasn't going to deprive himself of this little treat.

The other three all showed up about the same time and took their seats in the bureau's conference room. Robbie wanted to first find out what the others had learned. Bonner had found out that Maganelli was an officer in the three businesses LaBrock had mentioned. A quick credit check showed that Compsale had been in real financial trouble about the same time the State showed that Maganelli closed Cunningham Fuel Injection. Compsale had two officers listed; Maganelli and a James McGuire who listed a Los Angeles address on the State form. Maganelli and McGuire were listed as officers along with David and William Cunningham in Cunningham Fuel Injection.

Robbie stopped Vince right there and said, "There were four owners of Cunningham? LaBrock didn't mention that."

"There's one more thing. The State shows that at the same time Cunningham was closed in 2003, McGuire was dropped as a corporate officer in Compsale and replaced by Christine Maganelli," Bonner stated. Bonner finished by saying that the law suit which the Cunningham's had filed against Maganelli had been settled out of court.

"I ran checks on the Cunningham's. David Cunningham died right after the court settlement was filed and William Cunningham still lives in Plantation. I should have Maganelli's phone records for his home and cell phone on Tuesday," Bonner said.

"Do we know what the settlement with the Cunningham's was," Miller asked.

"No. The court documents were sealed and I haven't had a chance to do the legal stuff to find out anymore," Bonner explained.

"They got paid, so the business angle is not really a reason to knock someone off," Schultz added.

"Not unless Cunningham thought he got screwed," Robbie said.

"Yeah, but two years later?" Miller said.

"We need to go back and talk to LaBrock to see what else he failed to tell us," Robbie said.

Cappiello added what he had just learned from the others to the "white board "where he was recording all the pertinent information about the case. On one side of the board he had the known information. The pictures from the scene, notes he had made about the video tape and the list of players. On the other side, he listed the information he wanted to find out. At the top of that side of the board was a question mark which Robbie realized summed up his whole case.

He gave directions for Bonner and Schultz to find out what they could on William Cunningham and on their newest person of interest; James McGuire. The meeting broke up and the others left the office. Cappiello returned to his desk and began reviewing a few cases which he had pending to see if there was anything he could do on those cases, but decided he had better get home to limit his wife's anger over him not going shopping with her. He also decided that he would take Sunday off and take her to a nice restaurant for a Sunday brunch. He made a mental note to leave his cell phone at home.

Cappiello started Monday off with a briefing for his captain and the mayor. He was careful about what he told the mayor. He didn't want his suspects knowing he was looking at them via the news at noon. Miller was setting up another meeting with LaBrock and they were going to pay Cunningham a visit. Bonner was getting cell phone records from a contact he had at the cell phone company and Schultz was contacting the Los Angeles Police Department to see what they had on McGuire.

Cappiello and Miller headed back to Compsale. They were led into LaBrock's office and had to wait for him to finish a phone call.

"We have some more questions about Mr. Maganelli's business dealings," Robbie stated.

"Sure, ask me anything," Labrock answered.

"Let's start with McGuire. You failed to mention anything about him in our first meeting," Cappiello said.

"You're right, I apologize. Jim lives on the west coast and I just assumed he didn't have anything to do with this."

"He was removed as an officer of Compsale. Was that by his choice or Mr. Maganelli's?"

"Here's what happened. Vince got behind on Compsale's bills trying to support Cunningham. He told both McGuire and the Cunningham's that they would have to give up their interests in the businesses if he was going to continue funding them with his own money. Vince played hardball and they lost."

"I would take it that McGuire was not happy about that," Miller said.

"No, but that's business."

"Whose idea was it to put Mrs. Maganelli on the board?" Robbie asked

"Vince's. He said that the business could get some tax breaks if it was a minority owned business. Christine had nothing to do with the business though."

"You said you made the arrangements with the new investor who had interest in cell phone towers. What were they?"

"Marshall Kent called from an investment firm who was representing a new cell phone company. They wanted to lease our towers. He wanted a meeting, but said he would only have a few minutes when he got here on Thursday. He asked for Vince's cell phone number and asked that he be ready to go first thing in the morning. He was going to meet Vince at Ft. Lauderdale International."

"This guy calls out of the blue and wants a meeting?" Miller asked.

"I checked this guy and his company out. They are big time investors in the communications industry. They called us on Monday. His office sent down a non-disclosure agreement for us to sign, we looked it over, signed it and faxed it back to them."

"One last thing Mr. LaBrock, just routine, but where were you on Thursday morning."

"I was coming back from a business trip to Orlando. My plane landed about 8:30 that morning. You can check with the airline if you want to."

"That won't be necessary. We will need you to give us what you have on McGuire and Kent," Robbie stated as he and Miller stood to leave the office.

"I'll have my secretary give you that information if you can wait a minute."

The two detectives stood in the lobby while they waited for the secretary to gather the information they had requested. Miller looked at Robbie and said, "How did our shooter know about this meeting. Sounds like Maganelli left the house at the same time every day, so how did he know that he would be leaving the house early on Thursday?"

"You can add Mr. Labrock to our list of suspects," was Robbie's reply.

"So now we're talking about a conspiracy?" Miller said.

CHAPTER 13

Miller and Cappiello pulled into the Ft. Lauderdale Police Department parking lot on Broward Boulevard after leaving Compsale. They had called and spoken to Sergeant Tim Myers of the Internal Affairs Division who was expecting them. They wanted to see Cunningham's "jacket" to see what type of cop he had been. Myers was waiting for them in the lobby and escorted the pair to his office.

"Here's his file," Myers said as he handed it across the desk to Cappiello.

"When did he leave Ft. Lauderdale," Miller asked.

"1994. He left to start a business. He was into racing and came up with something for race cars."

Robbie was leafing through the file and said, "This guy was pretty active. I see a lot of counseling forms and commendations in here."

"Active is an understatement. I worked with him in narcotics. He did some good work, but always seemed to be on someone's shit list."

"He was involved in two shootings," Robbie asked.

"Yeah, one was on Andrews Avenue if I remember correctly and one was just down the road from the station. That one he took a lot of flak over. Shot a guy who was going for his partner's gun, but the press played it up as if he shot an unarmed man."

"I seem to remember that one from the news reports. You know anything about him recently?" Miller asked.

"I know the business thing didn't work out and that he went to work for a company in Baghdad; doing personnel protection. I've heard from some people around here that he works at the Embassy and escorts the Ambassadors and VIP's around the city."

"I heard that they need some really special training for those jobs," Miller said.

"They wouldn't have had to train Bill up. He went to the Miami-Dade SWAT School and he kept up on his specialized training while he was here. Don't know how rusty he got while he ran his own business though."

Cappiello and Miller thanked Myers for the information and left his office. They drove out of the station's parking lot and headed west on Broward Boulevard, back towards Plantation. Robbie was going over copies of Cunningham's file which Myers had supplied. He counted 26 commendations and 52 counseling forms and civilian complaints. "Myers wasn't kidding when he said this guy was active," Robbie said out loud, but was actually just talking to himself.

Miller pulled into a driveway on Camellia Court, which was the address they had listed for Cunningham. Robbie dropped Cunningham's file on the front seat of the car and the two walked up to the front door. Laura Cunningham answered the door and was a little surprised by the two men who were holding police b adges in her face. Her first thought was that something had happened to Bill's parents who were elderly and lived in the area. She was somewhat relieved when they asked if Bill was home, but then b egan to wonder why they wanted to see him. She led them to the living room and asked them to have a seat while she went to get Bill in the den.

"There are two detectives here to see you," Laura said with more than just a little concern in her voice.

"They're probably here to talk to me about Vince," was Bill's response. Laura noted that Bill was not the least bit nervous over the fact that the police were there to question him and his voice had remained very calm which Laura found reassuring.

"What would you know about that? You weren't even here."

"Stop worrying. They're going to talk to everyone who knows Vince," Bill said trying to reassure his wife.

Laura had picked Bill up from the airport on Saturday. She told him about Vince being shot and what was being reported on the news. Bill had not lied to his wife when he told her that he had not "heard" anything about the shooting, because it didn't make the news reports in Vegas. They had talked a little about how they were both still pissed off at Vince on the ride from the airport and surmised that Vince must have really screwed someone over royally to get shot for it.

Bill walked out and after shaking both detectives' hands, sat down on the couch across from where they were sitting. He looked exactly as Cappiello had pictured him. Tall, muscular, short hair and had the bearing of a police officer. He would have been picked out as a cop in any crowd. His face however, was different than Robbie would have expected. He had seen pictures of the mercenaries, or PSD's (Personal Security Details) as they liked to call themselves. The ones he had seen were hard looking, chiseled details, square jaws and crew cut hair styles. Cunningham physically fit the mold, he was in extremely good shape, but his face was rather boyish. He had soft looking skin and round wire rim glasses with a hair cut that was a little longer than military regulation. Just looking at his face gave the impression that he was a college professor rather than someone who had been involved in the worst society had to offer.

"I guess you're here because of Vince getting shot?" Bill said.

"Yes, I understand that you and your brother were partners with Vince and it didn't end well," Robbie said.

"I would say that was a fair evaluation of what happened," Bill replied.

"Tell us what happened between you and Vince," Miller requested.

"Dave and I have known Vince since high school. We drifted apart after school; Vince moved up to New York and Dave moved away to Michigan. I became a cop at Ft. Lauderdale P.D., but Dave came up with a great idea for a business and he and I started looking for investors. I ran into Vince one day at the store, I told him about the idea, he liked it and backed the business."

"But it didn't go good and you and Dave sued him. What happened?" Miller asked.

"Vince was a micromanager. He made it impossible to meet his deadlines and we fell behind on the products unveiling. We found out later that he was taking money from his other business to fund our business. When he got behind on the payments to his creditors, he told them that one of our other partners, Jim McGuire had embezzled the money. He threw Jim under the bus to cover his own ass. He then forced Dave and I out, we sued him and settled out of court. I haven't seen him since."

"I understand that your brother died right after you settled with Mr. Maganelli," Robbie said.

Laura interrupted the conversation from the hallway where she had been listening in.

"Had they stayed with the business, Dave would have had the insurance to go and get checked out. He died of colon cancer about four months after the settlement." she said. The men sat in silence as she continued; letting the anger she felt about Vince show in her voice.

"Vince is an ass. He's managed to screw over everyone he has ever done business with. I'm not sorry someone shot him. He is the only person I have ever known who actually deserved it."

"Obviously my wife is still a little upset over the whole thing," Bill stated.

"Sounds like you had a real good reason to hate him," Miller said directing his question to Bill.

Bill had a slight smile on his face when he said, "I know where this is going. Don't forget, I was a cop. I left for Vegas on Wednesday and came back home on Saturday."

"Why did you go to Vegas," Robbie said.

"The business partner Vince had lied about, McGuire, he and I are still good friends. We meet up in Vegas every once in a while just to get away. I just came back from Baghdad and needed some time to unwind, so my wife was nice enough to let me have a "boys" night out."

"Of course you can prove you were in Vegas the whole time?" Miller asked.

Cunningham turned to his wife and said, "Laura, my Delta tickets are still on my desk. Can you get them for me please?"

"That won't be necessary Mrs. Cunningham," Robbie said as he stood up to leave.

"Vince was a real ass. No one liked him. You really have your work cut out for you," Bill said as he followed the detectives to the front door.

"Looks that way," Robbie said as he closed the door behind him.

Laura looked at Bill and studied his face. She had come to know that little smile she had seen on his face when he answered that last question. He had that smile when he knew something that others didn't, something that he was not going to share. It really pissed her off when he did it to her, but this time the smile was not directed at her for a change.

CHAPTER 14

Miller didn't say anything on the short ride back to the station. He already knew what Robbie was going to need. He would want to confirm that Cunningham and McGuire were in Vegas and even though he had the airline tickets, Robbie would want to know if Cunningham was able to catch another flight back to Florida. He would also want to confirm that McGuire had stayed in Vegas. Miller began to smile when he thought that maybe he should go out there and check out the information for himself. Miller caught Robbie looking at him. "You're thinking about going to Vegas and checking out his story aren't you?" Robbie asked with a little laugh. Robert Cappiello was a really good detective; he could almost read minds at times.

"Who's the attorney of record for Mr. Maganelli in the law suit with Cunningham? I want to talk to him about their settlement and find out a little more about these guys," Robbie said as they walked back into the detective bureau. Miller went directly to his desk and grabbed one of the files Bonner had left on his desk. "The guy's name is Anthony Potter. I guess you want me to set up an appointment," Miller said not expecting an answer. Steve grabbed the phone book from his desk drawer while Robbie picked up one of the forgotten files from his desk. Cappiello was still going through his back log of files when Miller said goodnight and went home for the evening.

Tuesday morning found the team back in the conference room. It was time to find out once again if they had been able to find the answers to Robbie's questions. Sandy was still trying to track down information on the bullet. She had been to a local gun store and even the owner said he had never come across such a projectile. He did tell her that it might be a "big game round" and had given her a source to find out. She had also contacted the F.B.I. ballistics lab in Washington and had faxed them the pictures and the specifications on the bullet. Sandy finished by telling Robbie she would get back to him as soon as she knew something more.

Schultz had the most interesting news. He had contacted Marshall Kent from LaPointe, Brewster and Smith or should he say Mr. Kent's secretary. It seemed that Mr. Kent was on vacation in Italy and as a rule he did not conduct business when he was traveling on vacation.

"She told me that she knew all of Mr. Kent's deals and appointments. She did not know of anything the firm was doing with Compsale and that Kent had no plans to be in Ft. Lauderdale last Thursday or any other day for that matter," Schultz said.

"What about the non-disclosure LaBrock mentioned that he faxed to the office?" Robbie asked.

"I asked her about that and she said she did receive the fax from Compsale, but had no idea what it was about. She left it on Kent's desk for him to look at when he got back."

"OK, I guess we have to go back and talk to Mr. LaBrock again. This is getting monotonous," Miller added.

"What about phone records?" Robbie asked, directing the question to Bonner.

"I'm getting the subpoena today to get the records for Compsale, LaBrock, Cunningham and McGuire. I made a list of the phone numbers off the cell phone our victim had with him at the time of the shooting. Most are to his home and to Compsale. The last one he received was from a cell phone with a Los Angeles area code at zero six fifty one the morning of the shooting. It looks like it might be a disposable phone with no way to trace it. No one answers when you call the number."

Robbie leaned back in his chair and rubbed his temple with his fingers while he stared at the ceiling. He was going over what he had just heard from his team. He let out a sigh once he realized what he now had and how hard it was going to be to solve this case.

Cappiello was still staring at the ceiling when he said, "That tells me that we're now looking for at least two, maybe three people who really didn't like our victim. I don't think this was a professional hit. I think our conspirators are coming from the group we already know about."

"Do you think this was over a business deal?" Schultz asked.

"I want to know everything there is to know about LaBrock, McGuire and especially Cunningham. I want to know what training he received and exactly where he was every minute he claimed to be in Vegas," Robbie added. The group knew this was their clue to leave the room and get started on Robbie's request. Robbie was still staring at the ceiling after everyone had left the room. "Why couldn't my last case be a simple one," he uttered to himself.

It would take a little time to get the phone records once the subpoenas were issued by the judge and Miller had also requested credit card and bank records for their list of suspects. This would also take some time to get. Robbie was now sure that he had the right players; he just needed the evidence which would prove it. He was an experienced investigator and he was confident that once he confronted one of them with the actual facts and proved that they were lying, he would break them and get a confession.

It wouldn't be Cunningham who would give up a confession. He had been a cop for too long and knew the same tricks of the trade as Cappiello. He would have to get more information on McGuire before he decided what to do in his case; however he still thought he was somehow involved. LaBrock would be the key. It now looked like LaBrock had set Maganelli up. He set up the deal that got Maganelli out of the house early, but if he was setting up this charade, why did he send off the non-disclosure agreement. All he would have had to do is get Maganelli to sign it and put it through the shredder. Why did he leave a paper trail that would raise questions? Cappiello's plan was simple; get LaBrock talking, offer him a deal and get him to roll over on the others. Robbie was sure he could do it.

Cappiello pictured his last meeting with LaBrock and couldn't get one image out of his mind. He thought LaBrock looked like a weasel. Not because he was a slimy businessman; he probably was. It was because of his facial features. He looked like a weasel. His face was narrow and long. That combined with his long, slender and pointed nose gave Robbie that mental picture.

A short time after the meeting, Miller came back and found Cappiello standing in front of the white board in the conference room.

"I'm trying to get in touch with a contact I have at the phone company to see if we can speed up the process," Steve said. Robbie didn't immediately answer, preferring not to lose his train of thought. The non-disclosure agreement was bothering him. Maybe Kent's secretary didn't know everything about her boss's business dealings?

Robbie did not take his eyes off the board as he said, "Go ahead and check out Cunningham's story about the airline tickets. Check the other airlines as well."

"I'm missing something here. We have a business manager who has been with the same guy for eleven years. LaBrock makes our victim out to be a tough businessman, but everything else we have so far indicates he was a sleazebag. The two people that we know of who have a reason to do him in have an alibi. Then there is this thing with the non-disclosure."

"Maybe LaBrock and Kent have something going on. I'll find out what I can about Compsale and see who gets it if Maganelli is no longer in the picture," Miller said.

"Set up a time to see that attorney; Potter," Robbie requested.

Robbie looked at his watch. He had a 4 pm meeting with the captain to talk about his retirement which he had mixed feelings about. Working for the Plantation Police Department was the only job he had ever had. He hadn't even had a part time job in high school or college. The department was as much a part of his life as his wife and kids were. What was he going to do around the house for the next twenty years; if he made it that long? He had read somewhere that the average cop retires at fifty-five and that the average age of death for a retired officer is fifty-six. He was not thrilled by those statistics and was somehow going to make sure they didn't apply to him. He was sure his wife had plans for them to fill their golden years, but he just did not see himself as a gardener or lounging on a cruise ship.

Captain Mike Reaves was sitting behind his desk when Cappiello knocked on the door and went in without waiting for a response. He made himself at home while the captain finished up reading some report he would need to deal with later. Robbie and Mike had gone to the police academy together. They had been on the same patrol squad their first year and had been partners until Reaves had passed the sergeants exam which took his career along a different path than Robbie's. He had worked for Mike for the past ten years as a detective and the past four as the lead homicide detective. Robbie had a lieutenant who he was supposed to answer to, but Lieutenant Cross had learned a long time ago that Robbie would "go over" his head and talk directly to Reaves anytime he had something really important.

"I'm not going to be far behind your fat ass getting out of here," Mike said.

"Shouldn't be hard to replace you, some rookie has more knowledge about the job than you do," Robbie joked.

"I was looking at your file. Do you remember when we stole Sergeant Thompson's patrol car and filled it with frogs?" Mike said.

"We would have got away with it if you hadn't dropped your damn name tag on the front seat of his car."

"I think what really pissed him off is that it was mating season. I don't know how they ever got all of that shit out of the interior," Reaves said.

"He's been retired for what, about eight years now. What's he doing?" Robbie asked.

"He had a stroke about two years ago. They're feeding him tapioca through a straw in some nursing home outside Orlando." *Terrific, now THAT's something to look forward to*, Robbie thought to himself.

The pair sat for a couple of minutes while Cappiello filled Reaves in on the Maganelli case and several others he had pending. He told him which cases were worth following up and which ones he thought should be closed out. He would get with Miller to bring him up to speed on the solvable cases just as soon as he had a chance. The conversation then turned to the retirement. Reaves was planning a retirement party at the local Sheridan Hotel and wanted a date from Robbie.

"I want to finish the Maganelli case. At least get someone behind bars before I go out on retirement," Robbie stated.

"What if this drags on? You might not get to arrest someone before you retire, so I still need to have an official date so we can get this paperwork started."

"I would imagine that within the month I'll have someone charged for the shooting. Make it December 1st for my retirement date just to be sure."

"The 1st it is then," Reaves said.

CHAPTER 15

Wednesday had come and gone without much movement on the Maganelli case. Cappiello was waiting on the court system and some secretary at the credit card company, who was most likely overworked and not sharing his sense of urgency to get him want he needed. He had stopped by the hospital to check on his victim. The nurse on duty in the intensive care unit said she was surprised that he had made it this long. She was also surprised that she had not seen more of Christine Maganelli. She had been a nurse in the unit for a long time and usually had to force loved ones to leave. Robbie wrote it off to his first impression of Maganelli's wife. Maybe she just couldn't handle the uncertainty of not knowing what was going to happen to him or her future, but from what he saw at their house, she should be set for life.

Robbie returned to the station and made a few phone calls to local pawn shops to see if some items from a burglary he was working on had been pawned yet. He also called to follow up on a woman who had been beaten by her husband to see if her restraining order had been filed. He did manage to spend his lunch hour at home with his wife and his eldest daughter who was there with two of his granddaughters. He loved his four grandkids. He liked to play with them and really liked to spoil them. He bought them things that he knew would piss off his two daughters who would then have to deal with it once they left him. What he liked most however, was the fact that when they were done playing, the grandkids would be going back to their own homes and he could relax in peace.

His daughter, Betty was full of ideas that he and Sally could do once he retired. They sat at the kitchen table and listened to her grand ideas for their retirement. She had already contacted a travel agent who was making suggestions about a cruise on the Mediterranean. He could just see the conversations at the evening dinner table with the other old farts. He would have to listen to them talk about their exciting lives as accountants or stock brokers and would have nothing in common with any of them. Oh joy.

He knew nothing was going on at the station which would help him solve his case, so he took the opportunity to grab a quick nap before returning to the station. That was the good thing about being the senior detective; no one made you account for your time. As he drove back to the station, he received a cell phone call from Miller who had set up an appointment with Potter for the next morning. Robbie could only hope that maybe he could share something that would help solve this puzzle.

Cappiello canceled the usual morning meeting on Thursday so he could meet with Potter. Potter's office was on the sixth floor of an office building on North Federal Highway. He and Miller walked into an office which looked just like they would have expected from a high dollar corporate lawyer. All the furniture was real wood; mahogany to be precise and the chairs were high backed red leather. Potter sat behind a massive desk that could have sat eight comfortably for dinner. He was an older man, mid sixties Robbie estimated, but tall and thin and in good shape for someone his age. Potter motioned for the detectives to be seated at his conference table.

"I understand from talking with Detective Miller yesterday that you are trying to tie up some loose ends in one of your cases," Potter stated.

"Unfortunately, we have more questions than answers right now and we're hoping you can help us out," Robbie said.

"I've been Vince's attorney since the early 90's. Please feel free to ask anything as long as it doesn't violate attorney-client privilege." Robbie loved that statement. This guy relied on Maganelli to pay the bills, but he's worried that he might say something that Maganelli wants kept secret even if that means not catching his shooter.

"We're mostly interested in Maganelli's dealing with the Cunningham's and McGuire. We know the basics from LaBrock of how they met and what happened to force them out," Miller stated.

"I'm sure John Labrock left some things out," Potter replied.

"We've talked to him twice and we still haven't got the whole truth," Robbie said.

"Vince can be a ruthless businessman. He really doesn't care who he steps on and Labrock is right there behind him covering up anything that doesn't look right. Did John tell you he had a criminal record?"

"What! We ran him, but nothing came up," Miller said surprised.

"That's because it's sealed. Vince spent a lot of money to get it taken care of."

"What was he arrested for?" Robbie asked.

"Embezzlement and fraud. He was a bank vice president in charge of commercial loans. John signed off on a bunch of shady loans which he then got kickbacks on. All the loans went into default. He did seven years of a fifteen year sentence."

"Why would Vince hire someone like that to be his business manager?" Steve asked.

"He's Christine's cousin. That's why Vince hired him and then spent the money to get the record sealed."

"LaBrock told us that he was contacted by a company in California who was looking to do business with Towercell. Was that some sort of scam?" Robbie said.

"Not as far as I could tell. Vince checked out the company himself; Lapointe, Brewster and somebody. Vince had me look over the non-disclosure agreement. It was standard boiler plate, so I advised them it was ok to sign. I went to send it to the fax number on the page after Vince signed it, but John took it from me and said he would take care of it."

"Tell us about the law suit with the Cunningham's. I would imagine they weren't too happy about being forced out," Robbie said.

"Vince was losing money. He blamed just about everyone for their product not being released on time. The product was complicated; a revolutionary fuel injection system which needed a lot of engineering.

Vince is not the most patient man in the world and I don't think he fully understood the problems which surround designing a new product as complicated as that one was."

"Where did he get the money?" Miller asked.

"Vince had a very successful computer sales business. He was taking the money from that company and putting it into Cunningham."

"We understood that he was not paying his invoices from his supplier at Compsales and ended up accusing McGuire of embezzlement to save his own skin," Robbie stated.

"I told you he was ruthless. That was about the size of it, but it was LaBrock's idea. He convinced Vince that he could end up with both companies and came up with the plan to force those guys out."

"I see that in the State's records that Mrs. Maganelli replaced McGuire as an officer in Compsale. Whose idea was that, Mrs. Maganelli's?" Robbie asked.

Potter gave out a small laugh. "No, that was Vince's idea. Christine is a stay at home mom. She doesn't get involved in any of Vince's business. He wanted a minority owner for tax reasons, so they put the majority of stock in her name and made her the president of the company."

Miller was busy taking notes and trying to keep up with the conversation, but he wondered why Mr. Maganelli would make such a change. "She's not involved in the company at all then?"

"Christine is a very quiet and shy. Vince is very strong willed and I think he sometimes bullies Christine. I have been to their house for parties and he treats her more like a servant than his wife. I don't believe that he's physically abusive, but he's definitely the dominate one in that relationship. To answer the question, no she's not involved."

Miller looked up from his notes and asked, "Do you know anything about this meeting Mr. Maganelli was going to when he was shot?"

"No, other than just looking at the non-disclosure. It must have been important though. Vince doesn't leave the house before 9 a.m. for anyone. Ask John, he set that whole thing up."

"Let's get back to the Cunningham's. I understand that they settled out of court. How much did they settle for?" Cappiello said.

"I'm not allowed to divulge the exact amount, but it was a fairly good chunk of money."

"Did they get paid what the company was worth?" Miller asked.

"That was the whole contention of the suit. Each side had a different opinion of what everything was valued at. In the end, Vince offered an amount and they took it."

"Was there ever anything else said; such as they weren't happy with the settlement?" Robbie asked.

"Not that I'm aware of. I know Dave Cunningham died shortly after we settled and I'm not sure what happened to Bill after that."

'You said that LaBrock had made a lot of the decisions or at least came up with several of the plans which initiated a lot of this. Is there anything in the business bylaws that would give him control if Mr. Maganelli is no longer around?" Robbie said.

"No, everything would go to Christine, but she wouldn't get involved with running the business. She knows the company would go out of business if Vince and John weren't running the show."

"If Mrs. Maganelli is as meek and timid as you say she is, couldn't LaBrock convince her to give him control of the company so she would continue to have a steady source of income?" Miller asked.

"I guess it could happen," Potter said as if he hadn't even entertained that thought. Robbie sat there quietly listening and thinking to himself that LaBrock was looking more and more guilty as Potter filled in the missing pieces of the puzzle.

"What happened to Cunningham when they closed? I would imagine that there were patents and equipment," Miller said.

"It was a mess. Vince sold the patents and walked away from most of the debts of the company. Everyone was laid off and it wasn't pretty. A couple of guys had left good jobs to work there, including, if I remember correctly a good friend of the Cunningham's."

"You said he walked away from the company's debts. Anyone upset about that?" Robbie asked.

"Most of the debt was inventory or equipment which was repossessed by the companies who sold it to Cunningham. There were several people who were very vocal about the company closing. The one who was friends with the Cunningham's wasn't the least bit pleased and the guy who was Vince's private pilot also got hung out to dry. He lost his job when Vince stiffed the air charter service he flew for."

"Can you give us their names?" Miller asked.

"No, but I can get them for you. I used the pilot myself a couple of times and have his business card at home. I can send the information to you later today. I'll see if my accountant knows the other guy's name."

Robbie thanked Potter for his time and the two detectives left the office. Cappiello and Miller left the law office and started back towards the station. Traffic was heavier than normal and Miller inched his way westbound on Sunrise Boulevard, cursing under his breath at every out of town license plate which was slowing down his progress. Miller came to a stop at a traffic light and looked over at Robbie. He could see that Robbie was working out all the possible angles in his head so he kept his complaints about the traffic situation to himself.

Cappiello now had some of the answers he was looking for. From the additional information Potter had supplied, he would now be able to build a circumstantial case against LaBrock. All he had to do was link him with Cunningham, who he was sure was the shooter. He was still however, confused as to why LaBrock had sent off the non-disclosure. Was he working with Kent to take over the business? With Maganelli out of the way, it sounded as if he would not have a problem controlling Mrs. Maganelli. He would have known about Bill Cunningham's police experience and maybe kept up with him when he went to Iraq. Robbie needed to finish connecting the dots before he could take this case to the States Attorney's office to get some arrest warrants. He would also now have to find out some information on the other people Potter spoke of who didn't like Mr. Maganelli and how they might fit into the puzzle. Was this ever going to end? OK South Florida, everyone who hated Vincent Maganelli please move to the right. *"The state would tilt on its side,"* Robbie thought to himself.

CHAPTER 16

The weekend had come and gone. Robbie found himself once again sitting at the head of the table in the conference room at the police station, waiting for the rest of his team to show up. They all came walking into the room about the same time with Miller bringing up the rear. He had his now customary tray of hot coffees carried on top of a box of Krispy Kreme donuts. He sat down next to Robbie, passed out his goodies and opened up his note book. Robbie looked around the room and noted that Miller was the only one who looked like he had gotten any sleep at all over the weekend. He directed his question to Schultz.

"What the hell did you do this weekend?" Robbie asked while looking at Schultz who appeared to be the most hung-over of the group.

"We all got together at my house for the U of M game and it got a little out of control. The party started up again on Sunday with the Dolphin game. I think we killed two kegs."

"How many were at this party?" Robbie asked.

"Six, no five, Miller didn't come back on Sunday."

Robbie continued to look at Schultz as he addressed the rest of the group. He wanted some answers on the information he was waiting on. He didn't care how hung over they were, he needed the information and he needed it now. Schultz and Bonner stared down at the tabletop, avoiding eye contact with Robbie. They had seen him in this mood before and knew they had better deliver. He had most likely worked through the entire weekend on this case and would have expected the same from all of them. Each of them respected Detective Cappiello and felt that they had somehow let him down. Robbie looked around the room and realized from the expressions on his team's faces that he had accomplished exactly what he set out to do. He could see that they were all feeling a bit guilty. They would now work their asses off to get this case solved.

Robbie filled them in on what Potter had told him and Miller, then went around the room asking for opinions and any information they might have on the case. Bonner had come up with a year book from Plantation High School and pulled the book out of his brief case. He had put yellow sticky notes on the pages containing the pictures of David and William Cunningham, Vincent Maganelli and even Jay Goldman. Miller then told Robbie that Potter had called in with the names he had promised. The pilot's name was Ken Martin and the other guy he had mentioned was Nickolas Schapone. Robbie, playing a hunch asked Bonner to see if the two newest names were in the book.

"Yeah, they're both here. All of these guys were in the same class." Bonner said as he slid the open book across the table to Robbie. Robbie first looked at the picture of Martin, and then flipped through the pages over until he reached the one with Schapone on it. He then looked at the pages Bonner had marked. Robbie thumbed through the book as if he was reminiscing about his own high school days. He realized that he was just a few years older than the people he was investigating and based on the year printed on the book, he had most likely dealt with them during his first years on the force. He didn't remember any of their faces, but wondered if he actually had dealings with any of them.

It was at this point that Sandy came rushing into the conference room. She was carrying several files and was obviously upset over something.

"The meeting's half over. Glad you could join us." Robbie said not hiding his feelings about Sandy coming to the meeting late.

"I just got off the phone with the F.B.I. and this case just got real weird, real fast." Sandy said dropping her files on the first table she came to.

"What the hell are you talking about?" Robbie asked.

Sandy took a chair and gathered her thoughts. "It usually takes a couple of months to get anything back from the F.B.I. I just sent them the information on the bullet and they called me this morning asking all kinds of questions and want us to send them everything we have on this case."

Robbie's full attention was now on Sandy as he said, "What the hell is going on? Is Maganelli someone special?"

"No, but the bullet is." was Sandy's response. "This is a custom made bullet from a guy in South Africa. You have to know someone who knows someone to even get in to talk to the guy. You tell him what you need and what's it for and he makes you something that will work in your application. This bullet was made not to fragment going through the windshield. The agent also told me that a bullet will deflect at a ninety degree angle to the windshield based on the angle at which it hits the windshield. Someone knew exactly what he was doing."

"Like a police officer with tactical training!" Schultz added.

"Exactly" exclaimed Robbie.

Sandy continued by saying, "The F.B.I. has had several murders that have used this type bullet and Interpol has had a bunch of them also. Basically they are used to assassinate someone. The F.B.I. is sending a couple of agents down here to take a look at our files."

Robbie looked at Sandy and said, "Can we get in touch with the guy who sells these things and see who he sold too?"

She shook her head and said, "No. The F.B.I. said he doesn't talk to anyone about what he does."

Cappiello was now, more than ever convinced that Cunningham had pulled the trigger. He had done a little research on the group of people who were now providing private security for the "Green Zone" in Baghdad. It was a multinational group of ex-military and police who filled the security positions that the coalition forces were unable to man. They escorted convoys which crisscrossed the country delivering supplies to the forces fighting the war as well as providing personal protection for VIP's who had to travel around the country. Generally, these "contractors" had a much poorer survival rate than the military had. Once they left the protection of the "Green Zone", they were on their own and needed to rely on their own training and equipment to make it back safely. After listening to Sandy, Robbie keyed in on one thing that he had learned from his research. There were a lot of South Africans working there as dog handlers in Baghdad and it was even money that Cunningham had met some of them who would know about this bullet maker.

Robbie directed Miller to stay on the credit card companies so he could get their records. He also wanted to know when Steve would be getting the bank statements and credit reports of those involved. He tasked Schultz to do the same thing with the phone companies. Cappiello was becoming anxious over the progress of this case. It was not going as he had hoped and he was well aware that his retirement date was quickly approaching. He was not going to hand this case over to Miller so he could become the lead detective. This case was his and he was going to be the one that signed the probable cause affidavit to have the arrest warrants issued. It was true that Maganelli was still alive, but according to the hospital that could change at any minute. He had in the back of his mind the fact that homicide cases which go longer than forty eight hours have a poor average of being solved. This case had long since passed that time frame, but he reasoned that this was a very complicated case which required more time; at least that's what he hoped.

As the room cleared out after the meeting, Robbie was once again standing in front of his white board adding the information he had just received. Miller was standing behind him and reviewing what Robbie was writing.

"Potter said that Martin was a pilot, right," Miller said.

"I wonder if he had access to a plane which could make it to Vegas and back," Robbie said.

"I'll check the local airports to see if they had anyone come in from Vegas before the shooting," Miller responded.

"I need you to get me those bank and phone records. We need to see if any of these people were communicating before the shooting."

"We know that the phone call which was placed to Maganelli's cell the morning he got shot was most likely a disposable phone. If they used one, wouldn't they have supplied them to everyone involved?" Miller said.

Good point, Robbie thought as he finally looked away from his board and said, "Let's hope not."

Miller stood in front of the board and studied Robbie's lines which made the connections between all the players more understandable. He noticed a triangle connecting LaBrock, Cunningham and Kent.

"Robbie. You think these three are in this together?"

"It's not a stretch of the imagination. LaBrock gets greedy and wants everything for himself. He might need some money to make things right with the creditors, so he teams up with Kent who is with a venture capital firm. He gets Cunningham to do the dirty work and they all sit back and reap the rewards."

"What about Mrs. Maganelli?" Miller asked.

"According to Potter, she's a figurehead. Wouldn't be too hard to manipulate her or even steal the company out from under her once Mr. Maganelli is out of the way."

Miller took one more look at the board then walked out of the office. Robbie began walking over to his desk and tried to decide what his priorities were going to be. He wanted to catch up on the cases he had on his desk since the Maganelli case was at a standstill and needed to decide which one to tackle first. Robbie picked up the oldest file in the pile and began reading the responding officer's report, but his attention was drawn to the noon news which was playing on the TV that was mounted on the wall in the detective bureau. He heard the announcer say that they would have more on the "gang land" shooting in Plantation right after their commercial break. Cappiello sat through the commercial for the new and improved baby diapers and the one for the lawyer's office who wouldn't take a dime until the victim received a settlement from whatever accident they were in. All the time he wondered who had spoken to the news reporter without clearing it with him.

Across town, Bill and Laura Cunningham were sitting in a sports bar near the Sawgrass Mall where they had spent the morning shopping. Their attention was also drawn to the same news brief. It was noisy in the restaurant, but they could still hear the news anchor. "An unidentified source from within the Plantation Police Department has confirmed that arrests in the gangland style shooting of businessman Vincent Maganelli are imminent. The source, who wished not to be identified has confirmed with NBC 4 news that they have several suspects who would be arrested shortly."

Laura had not talked to Bill about Vince's shooting since the detectives had been to their home. She still remembered that telltale smile Bill had on his face when he was talking to Detective Cappiello. It infuriated her when he did it to her, but the detective would not have known what was behind the smile even if he had picked up on it. They had been married for fifteen years and she had never known Bill to keep a secret from her; however she could understand how he wouldn't be anxious to tell her about his involvement in something like this. Her husband had always been easy going. Very few things had ever upset him and he had always been cool, calm and collected any time there had been an emergency. She knew it was his police training which made him that way. Laura had been afraid that going to Iraq would have changed him somehow, but when he returned, she saw the same man she had fallen in love with a long time ago.

Laura and Bill never discussed what he had done in Iraq, mostly because she just did not want to know. She was often times afraid for his safety while working and living in a war zone, but she managed to cope with the situation. Laura avoided watching the news while Bill was overseas because she really didn't want to know what actually happened there or the dangers he was facing on a daily basis. She had a certain image of her husband which she did not want to destroy, but deep down inside she wanted to find out if he'd been involved in Vince's shooting.

Laura leaned over the table towards Bill, so as not to be overheard.

"You know how I feel about Vince, but I need to know something. Did you have anything to do with it?"

"Laura, you know I'm a very good shot. If I wanted him dead, he would be," Bill said.

"Who do you think did it then? They said arrests are imminent."

"I think they are just trying to make someone nervous. They put out that type of information when they don't have anything concrete and want to see who makes a mistake. They'll have phones tapped and someone will slip up and call their partner in crime and say "Did you see the news. I think they're on to us". The next thing you know, you see the guy on the evening news getting put into the rear of a police car in handcuffs."

"So you don't think they are close to arresting anyone?"

"No, they're just grabbing at straws."

Detective Cappiello was furious. He was on his way to Captain Reaves' office before the news piece was over. He didn't wait to see who was in the Captain's office, he just barged in.

"Did you just see the news? Who in the hell let out that information? We're close to making an arrest! We don't have shit right now," Robbie yelled.

"Calm down. Yes, I saw it and I don't know who's responsible."

"I've got two, maybe three people who I think did this, but I still need more information before I can arrest someone. Now, they're most likely packing their bags for Brazil!" Robbie fumed, but he still didn't take the Captain's advice to calm down.

"Sit down and calm down. Let's figure this out," Reaves said.

Robbie went to say something, but the Captain pointed at the chair in front of his desk and Cappiello sat down before he said anything else. Robbie hoped that it wasn't anyone from his team. They were all good cops and he was sure they would have talked to him before talking to the press. No one else in the department would have known much about the case. *"Maybe it was that publicity seeking asshole in city hall,"* Robbie thought to himself. The mayor was always trying to make himself look good in the news. This shooting had not died out of the news like most cases of its type. There were usually a few days of sensationalized reporting, and then the public's interest in the case would go away when something else of interest took its place. This case just didn't want to go away. Maybe it was how the news had played up the shooting in the first place; "Local businessman shot in gangland style execution", or it might have been just a slow week for news.

"I can make a call to Channel 4, but they're not going to tell me who talked to them," Reaves said.

"I can't believe this shit. I've got a whole team working on this and it might all go away because someone can't keep their damn mouth shut."

The Captain didn't answer. He knew Robbie was venting, but he had a right too. Talking to the press about this type of investigation could jeopardize the entire case. The people the detectives had already talked to would now have the ability to revisit their actions to see if there were any loose ends they needed to tie up if they were worried about being caught. The Bahamian Islands were only sixty miles away. If they were now panicking over what was reported, they might just flee the country. Either way, it made the case just that much harder to prove.

Cunningham finished the last of the beer he had with his lunch and looked at his wife. She had not said much since seeing the news report. It was obvious to Bill that what he had said to Laura had not completely removed the doubt she had about his possible involvement in Vince's shooting. He was unsure if he should readdress the issue or just let it drop. She knew him too well and would know from his voice and his facial expressions that he was being evasive with his answers if she asked him direct questions. He decided to drop it for the time being.

CHAPTER 17

Detective Cappiello had the rest of the day and most of the night to stew over that news broadcast. He was still not over it the next morning when he walked into the daily meeting with his team. Robbie studied their faces as he sat down; looking for any indication that one of them had betrayed him. He was somewhat relieved when he didn't see anything that would have given them away.

"I assume you all have seen yesterday's news broadcast?" he asked. Miller looked around the table at everyone assembled and then spoke up, "We all talked about it yesterday. It wasn't any of us. We thought it might be PIO or the mayor." Robbie once again looked at the faces of each one of his team members individually and decided that what Miller had said was true. It hadn't come from his team. The damage was done, so he decided to move on and see what new information they had for him. "OK, let's move on. What do you have for me?" Robbie asked. Miller spoke first.

"As far as I can tell, Cunningham was in Vegas from Tuesday to Saturday. I have him leaving on Delta flight 1804 out of Ft. Lauderdale International and returning Saturday on Flight 2216. I don't have him using his credit card for a hotel, but he did use it at a couple of restaurants in Vegas on Tuesday and Wednesday and at two bars on Thursday."

"No hotel?" Schultz asked.

"No, but Cunningham used his credit card for dinner at the Mirage Hotel. I checked the Mirage and they did have a reservation for two adjoining rooms in the name of James McGuire from Tuesday through Saturday."

"Did you check to see if Martin or Schapone were registered there," Robbie said.

"I also threw in LaBrock and Kent, but no go. If they were in Vegas, they were at another hotel."

"Did you check any other airlines to see if Cunningham came back here?" Robbie said. Bonner spoke up and said that he had looked into that for Miller and the answer was no; Cunningham hadn't been booked on any other commercial flights leaving Las Vegas during that week. Bonner however, did have some additional information.

"I checked with the FAA for any private flights leaving Vegas which had a destination at any airport in Dade, Broward or West Palm Beach counties. They had only one that week which landed early Thursday morning at Boca."

"Any information on that flight?" Robbie said.

"It was a private jet; a Hawker 1000. Left Vegas at 7:30 p.m. Vegas time and landed at Boca at 2:48 a.m. Later that day, it made a return trip back to Vegas at 3:00 p.m. and landed at North Las Vegas Airport and 5:42 p.m. Vegas time."

"Do we know who owns it?" Robbie said.

"Anderson Investment. They have a corporate office address in Santa Monica, California, but the plane is based out of the airport in Vegas. I checked with the airport and the company leases a private hanger on the field."

"Let's find out why they made the trip and if Martin had anything to do with it," Robbie said.

Miller had opened his note book and started flipping through its pages. He had remembered something he had written down when Bonner mentioned Los Angeles. Robbie was asking Schultz a question when Miller interrupted.

"Do you have an address on Anderson Investment?" he asked Bonner.

Bonner hesitated while he checked his notebook for the answer. "It's 100 Wilshire Boulevard in Santa Monica; why?"

"I ran a check on James McGuire. His business, Integrated PC's is located at the same address."

Robbie stood up and walked over to his white board. He wrote down the name "Anderson Investment" on the board then drew connecting lines between it and the names Bill Cunningham, James McGuire and Ken Martin. He then circled the name "John LaBrock".

"I want every one of these names cross checked. I want to know how they know each other, where they were on the day of the shooting; I even want to know if they send Christmas cards to each other. I want something to take to the State's Attorney," Robbie said in a very angry voice. He wasn't mad at his team. He was mad because he was missing a piece of the puzzle which really irritated him. His time on the department was running out and he wanted someone put in jail for this shooting before he left.

They all knew the meeting was over. Each member of the team picked up their paperwork and silently left the room. Robbie motioned for Sandy to stay back and asked her if he could see the video tape one more time. He wanted to make sure that he hadn't missed anything on the tape.

She left the conference room and returned a short time later with Miller in tow. All three of them watched the video at regular speed, then in slow motion. The video did not play as a regular movie would have. To record longer portions on a tape, the machine only recorded every few seconds which left gaps in the footage. It was then that Robbie saw something that he had missed the first time around. The shooter was not in the clump of grass as he had first thought. The shooter was the clump of grass. The shooter had camouflaged himself using the plants found in the bed to disguise his location. It was then that Robbie realized the shooter was wearing a ghillie suit.

Robbie told Sandy to stop the tape and back it up. As he did, he stood up and walked over to the TV and leaned in close to the screen. He then asked her to start it back up.

"Stop the tape. Look right here," Robbie said as he pointed to a clump of tall grass on the screen.

Miller also leaned in closer to the screen and examined the area around Robbie's finger.

"See this clump of grass? Watch what happens," Robbie said as he pointed at Sandy to advance the tape.

"It's gone!" Miller said with a surprised yet inquisitive tone.

"That was someone in a Ghille suit. You need experience to construct something like that. You just can't go and buy one off the shelf. I know it's a long shot, but check Cunningham's credit card records to see if he bought anything from a company who sells ornamental plants; Lowes, Home Depot or any of the local nurseries," Robbie said.

"We can't put him in town at the time of the shooting. He's got a good alibi that we've checked," Miller said.

"I didn't like what I saw when we talked to him. He was too arrogant, like he knew something and was betting we wouldn't figure it out. He's our shooter. I'm sure of it. We just have to bust up his alibi."

"About the only way we're doing that is to go and see what we can find out in Vegas," Miller said.

"Let's try to solve this here first, without costing the city a bunch of money. We still have some people to talk to before I get you an airline ticket. Let's start with Martin," Robbie said.

Miller and Cappiello drove out of the department's parking lot and headed north towards Pompano Beach. The address they had on Martin was right on the Intercoastal Waterway. The Intercoastal is a waterway which consists of natural inlets, salt-water rivers, bays, sounds and artificial canals. It provides a navigable route for boaters to travel the length of the country without many of the hazards associated with traveling on the open sea. In South Florida, the waterway is lined with high dollar homes belonging to families like the Kennedy's or Vanderbilt's. Unfortunately, owning one of these homes in South Florida without having a famous name or a high income job usually meant some sort of association with an illegal activity; usually drugs and Martin was after all, a pilot.

The house they pulled up to was not what they had expected based on the location. It was a modest home with a ten year old Monte Carlo sitting in the driveway. Martin must have seen them pull up because he met them at the door and after seeing their badges invited the two detectives in. The interior reflected what the detectives saw on the outside of the house; modestly decorated in mostly sixties style furniture. Martin invited the pair to have a seat on a couch in the living room as he moved navigational charts from a chair for him to sit in.

"Sorry, I'm getting ready for a flight. What can I do for you?"

"We're investigating the shooting of Vincent Maganelli and your name came up. We would like to ask you a few questions," Robbie said.

"I heard that Vince got shot. What do you want to know?"

"We understand that Mr. Maganelli was responsible for you being fired from your job at South Florida Air Charters," stated Miller.

"Yeah, he didn't pay his bill. My boss thought we had worked something out so he could get out of paying his bill, so he fired me."

"How much was the bill?" Robbie said.

"Twenty one thousand!"

"Why did they let him run the bill up so much?"

"He was flying at least once a week and had always paid his bill on time, but then he just stopped paying."

"I guess you weren't too happy about getting fired? I mean, he was a friend of yours right? You knew him from high school," Robbie said.

Ken remembered what Cunningham had told him to do. Tell the truth; don't lie. That however, didn't relieve the queasy feeling he had in his stomach. He was very nervous because he had never had to talk to the police before. Martin wasn't sure if the detectives were able to tell exactly how nervous he was, but he was going to tell them exactly how he felt. "Yes, I knew him from high school and he was a friend, past tense."

"So I guess that you really didn't like him very much after he got you fired?" Miller asked.

Ken was nervous over the questioning, but that one hit a nerve. He was mad and he didn't care if the detective knew it. "You got that right. I hated the guy."

"Enough to shoot him?" Robbie asked with an accusatory tone in his voice.

"Yeah, just wished I had, but I was here at home."

"Can you prove that?" Miller asked.

"No. I was here by myself, but you can check with the neighbors. I didn't leave the house; my car was here the whole time."

"Do you own any weapons?" Miller said.

With that question, Ken shifted in his seat. He was now very nervous and hoped it didn't show too much, but he stuck to Bill's plan. "Yes, I have a rifle."

"Would you mind if we have a look at it?" Miller said.

"It's under my bed. I can get it for you."

"If you don't mind, I'll just go and get it myself," Miller said.

Ken showed Detective Miller to the bedroom and stood back as Miller reached under the bed and pulled out a soft sided rifle case. He unzipped it and looked inside. "A three-o-eight isn't it?" he asked.

"That's right. I bought it because one of the guys I fly for has a hunting camp in Montana and he invited me to come up and go hunting with him."

"We would like to take this rifle and test it" Robbie said.

"Don't you need a warrant to do that?" Ken asked.

"You can give us permission or Detective Miller can sit here with you until I can get in front of a judge to issue one."

"Go ahead and take it, but I want a receipt."

CHAPTER 18

Miller turned over the rifle to Sandy when they returned to the station, then went to his desk. There was a large envelope sitting on his desk with a post-it note stuck to the outside which read, "I picked this up for you. It's your bank reports. Schultz." Miller opened the envelope and saw that it was the bank statements for Compsale and Towercell. He glanced over the report until his eye caught one particular line which interested him. He then began studying the report and saw several line items which he highlighted. He took the report with him to the morning meeting. Miller started off the meeting with the information he had just discovered.

"I have some money transfers from Compsale and Towercell to an off-shore bank," Miller said.

Robbie was surprised by the news. "Really! For how much?"

"I haven't studied the entire report, but there were three transfers that were dated after Maganelli was shot, totaling five point six million."

"Million?" Schultz said in amazement.

"Million! Transferred to a bank in the Cayman Islands," Steve said.

"Why the Cayman's?" Bonner asked.

"They're better than a Swiss bank account," Miller replied.

Miller had worked in narcotics for several years and knew all about the banking system in the Cayman Islands. He then enlightened the group with his knowledge of the Island's history.

"In 1794, the Caymanians rescued the crews off of ten merchant ships, which has since become known as the Wreck of the Ten Sail. The ships struck a reef and ran aground during rough seas which were caused by a hurricane. Legend has it that as compensation for their generosity, King George III rewarded the island, which was a British colony with a promise never to introduce taxes. This created an ideal environment for businesses who wanted to avoid taxes and a banking industry that catered to them. Drug dealers eventually found out about the Island's strict banking disclosure policies and their money poured into the island. The Cayman's have a population of just over fifty two thousand inhabitants, but ended up with two hundred and seventy eight banks that don't ask or answer any questions about their depositors."

"I guess we're going back to see LaBrock," Robbie said.

About the same time this meeting was going on, Bill Cunningham had parked his pickup truck outside a fitness center on University Drive. The person he wanted to talk to was always at the gym on Wednesday mornings. He waited in the parking lot until he saw them exit the gym and drove up alongside as they started towards their car. Bill rolled down his window and told the person to meet him around back of the building. A couple of minutes later, their vehicles were sitting side by side.

"How's it going," Bill said as the other driver put their car into park.

"Are you sure this is a good idea. Maybe the police are following you."

"Don't worry. I was a cop for a long time. I know what to look for."

"Do you have it?"

Bill didn't answer, but handed the driver a small brown paper bag.

"I've made sure the money transfers went through and have the paperwork ready to go. If the police get nosey, I'll make sure they get a copy. Everything will look legit. I sign a lot of his papers, so if they check the signature it will be a close enough match. I'm sure they'll believe he signed it."

"Good. I expect that they will be talking to me again. Ken said they were at his house yesterday and left with the rifle. He saw them go over and talk to a couple of his neighbors, but he thinks everything is still ok. I'm sure they'll be asking me if I own a rifle too when that one doesn't match up."

"Will you need to talk to me anymore?"

"If I do, I'll just meet you here," Bill said as he smiled at the driver and then left the parking lot.

Throughout the morning, Robbie considered what he had heard in that morning's meeting and changed his mind about talking to LaBrock. He decided that if he was going to talk to him once again, it would be done in a more official manner. Robbie made an appointment with Dusty O'Farrell, an attorney with the Broward County State's Attorney's office for the next morning. He wanted to know if he had enough evidence to get a search warrant for the Compsale offices.

Dusty had started with the State's Attorney's Office in Case Filing right out of college which was about the same time Cappiello became a detective. Once O'Farrell had passed the Florida Bar, she was assigned as a criminal prosecutor in the Larceny/Fraud Division which is where she met Robbie. Over the next several months, she prosecuted numerous fraud cases which Cappiello had investigated. As Robbie moved into different assignments within the Detective Bureau, Dusty seemed to get assigned to the Division within the Prosecutor's Office that also handled Robbie's cases. Along the way, she became one of the office's best prosecutors. Dusty was finally transferred to the Felony Trial Unit just after Cappiello was assigned to homicide.

Dusty's physical appearance did not match her courtroom demeanor. She was in her late forties, somewhat overweight and possessed a childish face and grin. Quite honestly, she looked like a Sunday school teacher. She was however, someone you didn't want to cross in the courtroom. Her examination of defense witnesses was legendary around the courthouse. Dusty was known to bring even hardened criminals to the brink of tears with her relentless cross examinations. She also had one of the best criminal law minds in the office, but more importantly to Detective Cappiello, she liked to work with him.

Robbie spent the rest of the afternoon going over all of his evidence and making sure he had everything correct for his probable cause affidavit for the search warrant he was hoping to obtain. The wrong address or a misspelled name could ultimately cause the case to be retried or worse, dismissed. He spelled out in the affidavit the evidence in a logical order which supported his claim that LaBrock had been involved in the attack on Maganelli. He described how Labrock claimed to have dealt with Kent and how he had arranged for the early morning meeting. He continued by describing the circumstances surrounding the non-disclosure agreement. He finished with a description of Labrock's criminal history and that the company's funds were being transferred to an off shore bank. After reviewing the affidavit for about the tenth time, he decided that he had better go home to his wife.

Sally sat across the dinner table from her husband and was a little agitated with him. She had spent a couple of hours making homemade sauce for his pasta dinner and now he didn't even seem to want it. He barely even talked to her for a week; only answering her questions with one word replies and she was getting a little tired of it. She knew this Maganelli case was worrying him, but enough was enough.

"Something wrong with dinner?"

"No, it's fine."

"How was work today?"

"Fine!"

"Ok! That's it. Either you stop ignoring me or you can find someplace else to sleep." That will get his attention she thought to herself.

"I'm sorry dear, what?"

"Robbie, you have been sitting around this house night after night and you haven't said more than ten words to me in a week. Tell me what's going on."

Robbie looked over at his wife and knew that he was in trouble. She was pissed. He always tried to make it a point to not bring his work home, but this time he guessed he hadn't done such a good job of it. He knew he had better let his wife in on his problem.

"I'm nowhere on this case. I'm getting a search warrant for the business to see if the manager was involved, but I am not connecting the person who I know did the shooting to the victim."

"You have never let a case bother you like this one."

'I know. I want this arrest as badly as I wanted to solve the first case I ever had. It's like this one will define my career. I don't want to go out with an unsolved case hanging over me."

"Honey, I told you before that everyone knows what type of detective you are. You may have to face that you're just not going to solve this one. Then what? You won't talk to me anymore while we're cruising around the world with all those people you'll have nothing in common with," she said sarcastically.

"I'll agree to talk to you if you'll promise no cruise ships."

"Why can't you get enough to arrest the shooter?"

"He's good, but he's arrogant and I hope that is what does him in. He's a former cop with some special training. He has an alibi, but I think it's bullshit. I just haven't been able to prove that he's lying. I'm hoping that this search warrant will turn up something that I can use against him or get his accomplice to talk."

"How's the victim doing?"

"He's alive, but just barely. He's still in intensive care, but if he makes it he'll be paralyzed for life."

"Robbie, you've done all the important work on this case. Even if Miller ends up taking over and makes the arrest, it will still be based on the work you've already done. You can still leave having the satisfaction of knowing that if it wasn't for your insight on this case and how you trained the guy who's going to replace you, there would have been no arrests."

Sally was right. He had trained Miller and anything Steve did to finish up the case would be a direct reflection on him. Robbie felt a little better about everything now and took a second look at his meal. He really did love the sauce his wife made for him and ended up having seconds.

CHAPTER 19

Bill sat in the driver's seat of his pickup truck sipping a sweet tea while he half listened to a Moody Blues song on the truck's radio. He was thinking about how many hours he had parked his butt in a car during the hundreds of undercover operations he'd worked while he was a cop. The saying was true, especially working narcotics; seven hours and fifty five minutes of boredom and five minutes of sheer terror. He had learned to control the terror and had actually come to look forward to it. The more he worked undercover, the more he'd come to realize that he could not wait for the shit to hit the fan so he could experience that rush of adrenaline. When he began to see that this addiction was beginning to affect his job, he left. He did miss the rush however and he was sure that needing to feed his cravings was part of the reason he had gone off to Iraq.

His attention was drawn to a group leaving the gym and he started his truck and pulled from his parking space. He slowly drove past the group and saw that he had been recognized so he drove off to the far end of the parking lot and waited. A couple minutes later a car pulled up alongside and its driver rolled down their window.

"Is there a problem?"

"No. Nothing we didn't plan for." Bill answered.

"I don't like meeting like this. What if the police are following one of us? Can't we just talk on the phone?"

"I told you, no phones. I've worked enough stakeouts to know what to look for and I needed to talk to you tonight."

Bill's companion nervously scanned the parking lot even though they didn't even know what to look for. After realizing that he was right, they turned their attention back to Bill.

"What's going on?"

"The friend I told you about in the State Attorney's office called and said that Cappiello had made an appointment to get a search warrant. Now don't panic, I planned for this."

Bill had contacted a secretary who he had once dated. She worked in the felony division at the States Attorneys office and processed warrant applications. Bill had used the excuse that he was following the investigation to see who had shot his friend. He knew that she still had the "hots" for him and he made some comments which lead her to believe that she still had a chance at him. She only knew there was an appointment to discuss the case but would let him know who's name was on the warrant when it came across her desk.

"Are you sure it's going to happen the way you planned?"

"Don't worry. There might be some arrests after they serve the warrant. I wasn't told what Cappiello was getting the warrant for, just that he had made the appointment."

Bill watched as the other driver continued to nervously scan the parking lot. Cunningham understood their uneasiness because this was the part of the plan that was out of his control. He had to rely on his knowledge of police work and knew how they did things at the State Attorney's office. Bill would now have to make some educated guesses which would keep the plan moving forward and him out of prison. After several moments of silence, the other driver spoke up.

"You've been right all along, but I sure hope you have this part figured out."

"As long as you have done what I asked, we will be ok."

"I've done everything you asked. The money has all been moved to the accounts."

"Remember this name, Kelly Dietrich. Don't write it down anywhere, just memorize it."

"Who's that?"

"He's one of the top criminal attorneys in the county and he owes me some favors. There will most likely be arrests after the warrant is issued. He's the best there is and will get whoever gets arrested out of jail the next day."

"Do you think I will get arrested?"

"It's possible. Just keep your mouth shut, don't answer any questions and call Dietrich as soon as they let you have a phone call. Don't worry; jail's not all that bad for one night."

Once again, Bill saw how nervous the other driver was becoming. He had worked with each person who was involved in his plan to make sure they understood how detectives worked and what was to be expected when questioned by the police. All he could do was hope that they believed in him and followed the script he had spent so much time developing. He was sure that people were going to be arrested and he might even be one of them, but he knew the system and how much evidence Cappiello was working with. Dietrich would have them out of jail the very next day.

"Dietrich does not come cheap, so I hope you put the extra money in the account I told you to set up here?"

"Yes. All the money has already been moved to the accounts we set up both here and in the Caymans."

"Are you sure you have done everything I have asked? What about the phone?"

"Everything is done and I got rid of the phone."

CHAPTER 20

The morning meeting did not produce any earth shattering information. Sandy had taken the rifle over to the Broward County Sherriff Office crime lab to conduct test firings on it. Each rifle barrel has distinctive marks left inside the barrel during manufacturing. These marks are transmitted to the bullet as it travels down the barrel. They are as individual as fingerprints. Even though they could not come up with the same bullet manufacturer, they were able to make a good comparison between a similar style test bullet and the one Sandy had taken out of the lady's wall. To her dismay, it wasn't a match. The two bullets showed different markings under the microscope. The markings on the bullet which were left by the lands and groves in the barrel showed that this weapon was not the one used in this crime.

The other bit of information which did nothing to help solve the case was that Cunningham and McGuire had made several phone calls to each other, but all were made before the shooting. Neither one had talked to the other by phone since then. As a matter of fact, none of the people on Cappiello's white board had talked with one another since the shooting. Robbie found that a little odd. Five of these people had all been important players at one time or another in Maganelli's life. Why weren't there phone calls made between anyone in the group after he was shot if for no other reason than to gloat? *"Just one more thing about this case which is puzzling."* Robbie thought to himself.

Miller did have one new bit of information which might turn out to be something. Steve had talked to the registered owner of the plane which was flown into Boca the morning of the shooting. He spoke with Thomas Barnes who had told him that he had sent the plane down to Florida to pick up a shipment of wine which was brought in for him from Chile.

"You'll never guess who his partner in making the wine purchase was."

"Don't tell me, McGuire," Robbie said.

"You got it. Barnes sounded very surprised when I asked him if he knew McGuire. Seems like they're old friends and do some business together. They went in together to buy this wine. They had another friend who lives in Boca buy the wine for them from a high end winery in Chile. He flew it up on his plane and Barnes sent his down to pick it up."

"Must be nice to have money," Bonner said.

"Just out of curiosity, what did they buy?" Schultz asked.

Steve checked his notebook and said, "A Concha y Toro Carmín de Peumo Carmenère. If I'm pronouncing right. A hundred and twenty bucks a bottle. I think he said they bought thirty cases."

"Like I said, it must be nice to have money," Bonner said.

"You asked him if they had any passengers, right."

"I did. He didn't know, but he gave me the name of the pilots and their phone numbers. He said they were on a trip until Monday, but I could talk to them then," Miller said.

"This is just a little too coincidental. Let's look a little harder at Barnes and McGuire," Robbie said.

Robbie looked at his watch and realized that he needed to get a move on if he was going to make the 10 a.m. appointment with Dusty. He grabbed the file containing the probable cause affidavit and the notes from his desk and headed out the door. After the thirty five minute drive to downtown Ft. Lauderdale, he walked into Dusty's office and saw that she already had a cup of coffee waiting for him on her desk.

"What have you got for me," she asked Robbie.

"I need a search warrant. A shooting we had in Plantation. Business guy named Maganelli."

"I've been following it on the news. I should have known it would be yours."

Robbie took a sip of the coffee and began explaining his case to Dusty. She made notes on a yellow legal pad as Robbie gave her the important points about the case. He wanted the warrant to cover any papers between LaBrock and Kent as well as any information on the money transfers.

"Do you know how they communicated?" Dusty asked.

"We have a couple of phone calls placed from Compsales to LaPointe, Brewster and Smith and to a cell phone with a Los Angeles area code, but we haven't found out whose number that one is yet."

"Ok, let's also add LaBrock's computer and any cell phones you find. I'm going to have to limit the search to his office since that's the most likely place he would have done any of this." Dusty was being careful. She wanted to make sure that the warrant was not too broad in its scope to ensure that it would be difficult for a smart defense attorney to challenge later on.

Dusty prepared the search warrant and they went to look for a sympathetic judge to sign it. They located Judge Roberts and after Dusty had given him the "Reader's Digest" version of the case, he signed it after having Robbie swear under oath that what he had presented was factual. Dusty reminded Robbie that he needed to return the warrant after it was served, but he just stared at her with a slight look of disbelief on his face. He couldn't remember how many warrants she had done for him, but this was definitely not his first rodeo. He responded to the request by offering to buy her lunch at the court house's coffee shop, but she said that she needed to prepare for that afternoon's court case. She was before Judge Finch and he didn't like any mistakes or delays in his courtroom. With that said, Robbie picked up his paperwork and headed back to his car.

Robbie called Miller from his car and told him that he would pick him up at the station in a half hour. He wanted to go over to Sunray Machining in Lauderhill and talk to Schapone.

Cappiello and Miller waited in a conference room at Sunray for the manager to go and get Schapone. He was none too happy about taking Nicky off of a machine, but realized he had no real choice in the matter. He had a deadline to meet and this was not going to help him meet it.

Robbie listened to the loud hum of the machinery just on the other side of the wall and wondered how anyone could stand that much noise all day long. The volume of noise suddenly increased as the manager opened the door which leads from the office into the machine shop and escorted Schapone to where the detectives were waiting. He gave one last disgusted look at the detectives and left them alone with Schapone.

"We're here to ask you a few questions about Vince Maganelli," Robbie said.

"Go ahead, ask me anything," Nicky said.

"We understand that you knew him in high school and you at one point worked for him," Robbie asked.

"Let's get one thing straight. I worked for Bill and Dave Cunningham, NOT for Vince."

"Doesn't sound like you liked him much," Miller said.

"No not really. I knew him in school, but he turned out to be an asshole."

"But you went to work for him," Robbie said.

"I told you, I didn't work for Vince, I worked for the Cunningham's. Vince was just the guy who paid the bills. He had no clue what was going on or what it took to produce that system. He just came in to the shop and yelled a lot."

"When did you leave?" Robbie said.

"I was fired. After he got rid of Bill and Dave, he fired me. I guess he didn't want a snitch in the shop to report back to Bill and Dave what was going on in the company."

"I guess that pissed you off," Miller said with a bit of an attitude.

Nicky was becoming agitated at the questions and nervous at the same time. He knew it showed, but he trusted Bill and did exactly as he was told to do. Bill had told him that they would talk to anyone who had a problem with Vince in the past and that he shouldn't be surprised if they came to talk to him. Bill had reassured him that having detectives talk to him didn't necessarily mean they knew anything about his involvement in the shooting. They would check him out before the interview and they might even learn about the van. Cunningham had prepared him for today's interview by explaining how the detectives would talk to him and how he should respond. He kept remembering the one point that Bill had emphasized; don't lie or make up something that they could check.

"Yeah, it did. I left here to go over there. I busted my ass, worked a lot of overtime to get things rolling and he fired me."

"We ran a check and found that you registered a Chevrolet van last September," Miller said.

"That's right. I bought it for a company I have on the side. I do some machining for people and I needed it to pick up supplies and make deliveries."

"You still have it?" Robbie said.

"No. It was a piece of shit. The motor was bad and it was going to cost more than it was worth to fix, so I sold it to a salvage yard."

"When?" Miller asked.

"The day Vince got shot. I remember hearing about the shooting on the radio when I was driving over to the salvage place."

"What's the name of the salvage yard?" Steve said.

"All Pro I think it is. It's on State Road 7, just north of Griffin."

"Ok, thanks. I don't think we have any more questions. Make sure you thank your manager for us. I don't think he liked us being here," Robbie said.

Nicky walked the detectives to the door and took a deep breath as he watched them get into their car to leave. He knew his nervousness showed, but Bill had told him that would be a normal response. People are always nervous when the police showed up unannounced to question them. He sure hoped Cunningham was right as he turned to go back to his machine.

"That guy was nervous," Steve said as they pulled out of the Sunray parking lot.

"I'm not sure how to read that. Maybe we just intimidated him," Robbie said.

"Why don't we go over to that salvage yard before we head back to the station," Miller said.

The two detectives walked into the "showroom" of the salvage yard. The place was scattered with piles of car parts and stacks of boxes containing more parts. They walked up to the counter and noticed one guy sitting behind a desk which was covered in invoices and what appeared to be his chicken dinner. He looked up at the pair without saying a word and began licking the chicken grease from his fingers. He finally stood up, pulling his pants back up in the process and walked over to the counter where the detectives were standing.

"You need some parts?" he asked.

"No. I'm Detective Cappiello and this is Detective Miller from Plantation P.D. We have some questions about a van which was brought here recently."

"Man. I don't take in stolen shit. I check the VIN numbers and the title before I buy anything," the man said is a real brusque voice.

"Calm down Terry. We're just here to check out the van to see if it was used in a shooting. That's all," Robbie said. He was just assuming the man's name was Terry, because that was the name printed on his blue work shirt.

Miller then gave "Terry" the date the van was turned in and Schapone's name so he could check the company's records.

"I've got it right here," Terry said as he pulled a file from the filing cabinet.

"It's titled to Nicholas Schapone with a Davie address. Got the copy of the title right here. We paid two fifty for the thing."

"Where is it now?" Miller asked.

"We set it out to be crushed. Not much call for van parts. We pulled the engine and trany, took the tires off and some other parts we could sell."

"When did you send it out to be crushed?" Miller asked.

"Don't know exactly, but I've got the pictures of the van here in the file."

Terry then handed over several Polaroid pictures which showed all four sides of the vehicle. The detectives paid particular attention to the front view of the van. They noticed the multicolored front end which was very different from the all white van they were looking for.

"Is this the way it came in," Robbie inquired as he showed Terry the picture which had the front of the van on it.

"Yeah. I take the pictures as soon as we buy them just in case some insurance guy or a couple of cops show up looking for a stolen car."

"Thanks," Robbie said as he handed Terry the pictures and turned to leave.

CHAPTER 21

It was a little past nine in the morning when Cappiello, Miller, Schultz and Sandy walked into the Compsale offices. They walked right past the receptionist and straight for LaBrock's office. Linda, the receptionist immediately jumped up from her chair. She yelled at the group, 'Hey, you can't just go in there" as she followed, trying to keep up. None of them paid any attention to Linda and entered LaBrock's office without stopping. LaBrock, in a very sarcastic tone said, "Can I help you?" Robbie placed the search warrant which he'd been carrying in his hand on LaBrock's desk in front of him.

"We have a warrant to search your office."

"What are you talking about? This is bullshit! Linda, get Potter on the phone right now and tell him to get his ass down here right away."

"I don't care what she does, but you're going to go out there and take a seat along with Detective Schultz," Robbie said as he motioned for Schultz to take control of LaBrock and escort him from the office.

"You damage anything in there and I'll have your asses," LaBrock raved as he left his office.

Robbie looked around the room and decided how he wanted it searched. He walked out of the office and said to LaBrock, "you want to give me the password to your computer or shall we take it with us to the station for the computer geeks to tear apart?"

"Go fuck yourself!" LaBrock yelled.

"I'll take that as no," Robbie replied as he turned to go back into the office.

"Sandy, you take care of the computer on his desk and anything electronic. Don't forget about the memory sticks if you find any. Steve, you take the credenza over there and the book shelf. I'll take the desk."

All three then began the task of systematically looking through their assigned areas. After a few minutes, Miller pulled out a file which he noticed was marked "Wire Transfers – October". He called to Robbie who walked over and began looking at the open file. Miller checked his notebook and pulled three pieces of paper from the file. Each one corresponded with the dates he had seen on the banking statement. He then pulled out two more which showed that another two and half million dollars was transferred after he'd received the information from the bank. Robbie picked up the papers and went out to talk to LaBrock.

"Can you tell me about these," he asked as he showed the papers to LaBrock.

"Is that what this is about? You've made a big mistake. I have a paper from Vince that states that I am to transfer the money from our savings accounts into those off shore accounts should anything happen to him which might be life threatening. He's in intensive care with a bullet hole in him. I'd say that was life threatening, wouldn't you?"

"You say you have a paper which authorizes these transfers?"

"Yes. It's in that same file."

Robbie turned to go back into the office, but was met at the door by Miller.

"Look what I have," Miller said as he held up a cell phone.

"Where did you find that?" Robbie inquired. Before Miller could answer, LaBrock jumped out of his seat and in a very excited voice said, "Wait a minute. That's not mine. What the hell are you trying to pull here?"

Miller looked at LaBrock and said, "First of all, sit back down before I'm forced to help you find your seat". LaBrock looked at the two detectives who were now towering over him and decided not to push the issue. He reluctantly sat back in his chair. Miller continued by saying, "I found it in the bottom of the credenza, hidden under some paperwork and guess what, there have been three calls made from this phone. One of the numbers is Maganelli's cell phone and the time shows that the call was made just before he was shot."

"That's impossible! Someone's trying to frame me," Labrock yelled out.

Robbie walked over to where LaBrock was sitting. He grabbed him by the arm and pulled him up from his chair. Schultz grabbed the other arm and held on while Robbie pulled out his handcuffs. Schultz glanced over at Robbie in amazement. He didn't even know that Robbie still carried handcuffs. Robbie pulled LaBrock's arm down and positioned it behind his back. As he did so, he placed the cuffs on LaBrock's wrist and said," Mr. LaBrock, I'm placing you under arrest for the shooting of Vincent Maganelli. You have the right to remain silent." Robbie continued with the Miranda Rights which he could recite from memory, but LaBrock wasn't listening. He continued to tell the detectives who were now confining him that he was innocent and that he was being framed. They however, weren't listening.

After Robbie had finished with the formality of the Miranda Warning, he had LaBrock sit back down in his chair. He looked around and saw the office staff staring at what was unfolding before them in amazement and whispering among themselves. LaBrock yelled over to Linda to once again call Potter to "Get his fucking ass down here!" Robbie left LaBrock with Schultz and went back into the office. Sandy had finished packing up LaBrock's computer and Miller had found the letter of authorization LaBrock had mentioned. He had also found some papers which had been signed by Maganelli which he took, so a comparison of the hand writing could be made.

Sandy and Miller made a couple of trips out to Sandy's van carrying the items they had just collected, which were all placed in evidence bags. Each item was documented with the case number, date and victim's name so they could be stored properly in the evidence locker down at the police station. When she finished, Miller and Schultz escorted LaBrock from the building and placed him in the rear of Robbie's car. LaBrock sat silently, with Miller sitting alongside of him during their trip back to the police station.

When they arrived, Miller escorted LaBrock up to the Detective Bureau while Robbie parked the car. He had already started filling out the arrest affidavit when Robbie walked into the office. Miller had put LaBrock in one of the Bureau's holding cells which is where Robbie found him. Cappiello then removed him from the cell and took LaBrock into one of the interrogation rooms. Miller went over and turned on the video recorder which would give them a complete history of everything that was said in the room as well as proof of his treatment should LaBrock claim that he was intimidated or worse; beaten while in the detective's custody.

Miller had removed the handcuffs from LaBrock when he placed him in the cell and Robbie saw no reason to put them back on for the twenty foot walk over to the interrogation room. Robbie pointed at a chair on the opposite side of the table from his and motioned for LaBrock to take a seat. Robbie went through the formalities again of reading LaBrock his rights and asked if he needed a lawyer.

"Potter should be on his way over here," LaBrock said.

Robbie pulled a piece of paper from the file folder he was carrying, placed it on the desk and slid it towards LaBrock. "Is this the authorization you claimed Mr. Maganelli gave you to transfer the money into the off shore account."

LaBrock had seen all the police shows where the bad guys always asked for an attorney as soon as they as they entered the interrogation room, but he didn't see any problem in answering that question. Basically because that was exactly what it was. "Yes, that's it, but Vince didn't give it to me, Christine did."

"When did she give it to you?"

"A couple of days after Vince was shot."

"Did you know it existed before she handed it to you? It seems a little convenient that he gets shot and she's giving you a letter which says to move his money to another account."

"That's the way Vince did things. He has a contingency plan in place for just about anything you could think of and I didn't always know about them before he would spring them on me. I've seen his signature a hundred times. I looked at the signature on the paper and it was

Vince's, so I sent the money where he wanted it to go."

"Why move the money to an off shore bank?"

"Like I said, Vince had things going on that even I didn't know about. He did this type of stuff all the time."

"Tell me about the cell phone."

"It's not mine. I have no idea where it came from."

"We'll get back to the phone. I know you didn't shoot Maganelli because we checked your alibi and confirmed you were on the flight you said you were on. I want to know who you're working with. You talk to me now and we can make a deal; you wait and I find out who else you're working with and they might get the deal."

"I have no idea what you're talking about. I am not "working" with anyone. I didn't have anything to do with Vince getting shot."

"You set up the meeting. We have the phone you used to call Maganelli to get him out of the house early, then there's your criminal record. You need to tell me who you were working with. It will go a lot easier on you if I hang this on the shooter. You help us, testify against your partner and I'll recommend to the prosecutor that you get the minimum sentence."

"I didn't have anything to do with…" LaBrock stopped right there. He decided that he had said enough. "I think I want to stop talking until I can talk to my attorney."

Robbie didn't say anything more. He stood up, took LaBrock by the arm and led him back to the holding cell so Miller could finish filling out the arrest affidavit. Robbie had hoped that LaBrock would see things his way and realize that he had him cold. The only way he was going to avoid a long prison sentence was to cooperate. If LaBrock thought he was going to get out of this some other way, he was wrong.

When Miller finished the paperwork, he handed it over to Robbie for review. He then made arrangements for LaBrock to be transported to the county jail, so he could be processed and then wait for his arraignment before a judge in the morning. Robbie called Captain Reaves and advised him of the arrest, and then he called home. He wanted his wife to know that at least some of the pressure he was feeling had just been relieved.

When Robbie left the building to go to his car, he noticed several of the local news trucks parked in the parking lot. The reporters had all set their cameras up near the front door of the station. Captain Reaves, the chief of police and the mayor were standing in front of the main entrance conducting an interview which Robbie had declined to be a part of. He watched as the reporters tried to get the mayor's attention so they could ask him their questions about this big time arrest. Robbie noticed that the mayor was reveling in all of the attention he was receiving from the reporters; like he had anything to do with the arrest in the first place. Robbie shook his head and gave out a little laugh as he entered his car and left for home.

Robbie knew something was up when he walked into the kitchen when he got home. Sally had the radio on and was humming to a sixties tune by Neil Diamond. She was standing by the stove and cooking something which smelled really good. He looked over into the dining room and saw that the table was set up for a formal dinner.

"What's going on? Are we having company?" Robbie asked.

"Nope! Just the two of us. We're going to celebrate."

"Celebrate what?"

"You being the best detective in Plantation. We're going to have an Italian dinner, complete with a nice bottle of wine and cannoli's. If you play your cards right, you might even get lucky tonight."

"I should make this type of arrest more often."

Robbie sat down at the kitchen table and was enjoying watching his wife move around the kitchen. She was so happy; she seemed to be floating as she moved from one point to another. Robbie realized that he had not seen her this happy in a while and also realized that it was because of him she had been depressed. He offered to help, but was told to sit and wait. Robbie reached over and used the remote to turn on the television which was sitting on the kitchen counter. The "News at 5" was on and he was somewhat surprised that his arrest was the second story. "It must have been another slow news day," he said out loud. Sally didn't hear him, she just kept moving around the kitchen getting what she needed to complete her masterpiece.

"Plantation police arrested John LaBrock this morning in the gangland style shooting of businessman Vincent Maganelli which occurred earlier this month," the news anchor said as they showed a short clip of LaBrock being led from the station in hand cuffs. They then showed LaBrock being placed into the rear of a waiting patrol car which then drove away. Robbie had seen this same scene portrayed in so many different arrests that he thought to himself that reporters must be taught to film that sequence of events in "How to be a Reporter, 101" in college. The anchor then said that the police were going to make more arrests in the coming days. The news report then cut to a piece in which the mayor was telling the assembled reporters how diligently his detectives had worked on the case and that more arrests were on the way. "Pompous ass" Robbie muttered.

"Sorry, I didn't catch that." Sally said from the other side of the counter.

"Nothing. They just had the mayor on talking about the arrest. As usual, he sounded like a jerk."

"Did you get mentioned?"

"Nope, just Reaves and the mayor." Robbie clicked off the television because he knew all six local stations would be carrying the same news report. He really didn't want to see the mayor on TV any more than he had to. Robbie got up and went over to give his wife a hug. She slapped his hands as he reached around her to get a small taste of the sauce she was stirring. "You can wait," she said. He just smiled at her as he returned to his seat at the table, but not before giving her a parting little pinch on the butt.

CHAPTER 22

Robbie spent Saturday relaxing on the couch, watching college football games. Betty had brought over both of his granddaughters who decided they wanted to have "tea" with poppa. This unfortunately was happening during the University of Miami game which he had planned to watch, but he made the best of it. On Sunday, he had taken Sally to brunch, and then decided that the grass was a little too long and spent much of the afternoon taking care of the yard. All in all it was a relaxing weekend which he really enjoyed. *Maybe retirement won't be all that bad,* he thought to himself as he and Sally grabbed some snacks before sitting down to watch a movie for the evening.

Monday came all too soon and he found himself back in the detective bureau before anyone else. Although he had tried not to think too much about the case over the weekend, he just couldn't let it go. He'd been observing people his entire career and was an expert at reading body language. Watching LaBrock answer his questions on Friday made him think that maybe he was telling the truth. His body language said he was, but the evidence was against him. He could have just been a very good liar and everything Robbie had learned about LaBrock up to this point indicated that he mostly likely was. Robbie however, found it hard to dismiss the fact that the phone that was used to set up Maganelli was found in LaBrock's office. Why had he kept it? Why not just get rid of the evidence. Maybe for the same reason he had sent off the non-disclosure. It all didn't make sense. Robbie needed to find out what was his reasoning.

Cappiello pulled a file from the top of his pile. He noticed that luckily, the pile had not grown since he was assigned this case. He looked at the writing on the file's tab, "Maganelli, Vincent – Aggravated Battery". He opened the file and removed LaBrock's arrest affidavit which had the search warrant and evidence receipt for the items they'd removed from his office stapled to it. He had called Dusty after they had returned to the station on Friday and filled her in on what had happened. He was going to return the search warrant to her later today, after he took care of a couple of other things first.

He and Dusty had discussed on Friday how to make it difficult for LaBrock to get out of jail quickly. He would be sitting in jail over the weekend and would have his bond hearing around 9 a.m. that Monday morning. LaBrock would most likely have the means to afford bond, so Robbie wanted Dusty to try for the maximum allowed. She was going to cite the money transfers and LaBrock's criminal history as reasons for the judge to make the bond unobtainable. Better yet, she was going to argue that bond should be denied because he was a flight risk; at least that was how Dusty was going to present it.

Miller came in before the rest of the team and was carrying a police supplemental report in his hand.

"I've got Sandy's report on the phone we took out of LaBrock's office. There were only three calls made from the phone. The first was to a Los Angeles area code four days before the shooting. The second was to Maganelli's phone the morning he was shot. The interesting part is that there were no fingerprints on the phone. Why would LaBrock hide it in his own credenza after wiping it clean?"

"Just one more piece of the puzzle that's not fitting together," Robbie grumbled out loud.

"Oh, and there is one other thing that is going to piss you off," Miller said with a slight smile on his face.

What's that and do I really need to hear this," Robbie replied.

"That third number was a local call. I called it this morning to see who answered. It's NBC 4 in Miami".

"LaBrock called the news station? Did that son of a bitch pretend to be a cop and leak the information? What was he trying to do? Throw us off track," Robbie said with more than a little anger in his voice.

"I don't know. It makes no sense at all. What could he possibly gain from talking to the media?"

"This is getting unreal. He is either a total idiot or he's got some kind of plan going," Robbie said.

"Maybe he hung on to it to frame someone else. If he's in it with Kent, maybe they planned to plant the phone on Cunningham and then all of the evidence would point at him. I also have nothing on McGuire. No criminal record. No phone calls to anyone here. The only thing that's connecting him to this case is knowing Maganelli and having his name pop up with regards to a plane full of imported wine," Miller said.

"That's all just too coincidental for me. I'm starting to think that Kent had nothing to do with this. They just used him as unsuspecting bait. I'm starting to think that LaBrock had something set up with McGuire and Cunningham to somehow get the business away from Maganelli. A payback if you will for screwing them out of their business," Robbie said.

"That's a good motive, but LaBrock's lawyered up and I don't think we'll get anything out of Cunningham."

"Let's wait and see. LaBrock doesn't look like the type of guy who's going to do well in jail. Let's see what Dusty was able to do with the bond hearing' Robbie said.

"Do we know who his lawyer is yet?"Miller asked.

"No, but it won't be that guy Potter. He's corporate and LaBrock will need a good criminal lawyer to get him out of this one. I still think there are too many loose ends. Looks like you're going to get that trip to Vegas after all. You want to go with Bonner or Schultz?"

"Let me think about that one," Miller said with a smile on his face.

"Before you pack your bags, I want one more chance at Cunningham. He's egotistical and he might say something we can use."

Nothing of significance came out of the Monday morning meeting. Everyone was still getting pieces of information about bank accounts, credit card usage and trying to find out where all their suspects were at the time of the shooting. Robbie told the group what he now believed was the motive for the shooting and directed the group to concentrate on trying to tear holes in people's alibis. He wanted the credit card and bank statements gone over again; a third and fourth time if necessary. There was something missing and he was sure that his trio of suspects had overlooked some key part which would tie everything he had together. He just hoped his crew would know what it was when they finally found it.

Robbie was sitting back at his desk when the phone rang. It was Dusty and she didn't have the kind of news that Robbie was hoping for. The judge evidently sided with her and made LaBrock post a five hundred thousand dollar bond which unfortunately, LaBrock was able to make. If that wasn't bad enough, he was being represented by Kelly Dietrich; one of the top three criminal lawyers in the area. Robbie surmised that LaBrock had money and he was going to go through a lot of it hiring Dietrich. He required a forty thousand dollar deposit just to sit down and see if he wanted to take your case in the first place. He would not allow LaBrock to talk to the police unless it was in his client's best interest. Robbie hung up the phone and yelled for Miller to get their car.

It was late morning when Cunningham saw the unmarked police car pull into his driveway. He had been working in the garage so when Cappiello and Miller exited their car, he motioned for them to follow him into the house. Laura went shopping and wouldn't be back for a few hours, so Bill knew he could say things that would lead the detectives in the direction he wanted without causing him problems with his wife.

"Good morning, please sit down," Bill said as he pointed towards the kitchen chairs.

Bill sat down at the head of the table and said, "I saw the news. I guess congratulations are in order for your arrest."

"LaBrock is only one part of this. We are still looking for the shooter," Robbie stated.

"What can I do for you then?" Bill asked.

"We just need to verify a few things and ask you some technical questions if you don't mind."

"Sure, anything."

"We of course, checked your alibi. When you were in Vegas you didn't charge a room to your card," Miller said.

"That's right. Jim sprung for the room. I bought dinners and drinks.

"We want to ask you about two of the charges on your credit card," Robbie said as he pulled two photocopied pieces of paper out of his folder. He laid them on the table so Bill could see them.

"Here are two receipts from Thursday, the day Maganelli was shot. We looked at the signatures on these and compared them to other copies of things you signed. They don't look much like your signature. Can you explain that?"

Bill picked up both pieces of paper; one was from PT's Sports Bar and the other from Steiner's on South Las Vegas Boulevard. Cunningham had not actually seen the receipts before; Jim had only told him where he was going. *"Ninety two fifty at PT's and a hundred and seventy six twenty two at Steiner's. Damn, looks like he had a good time."* Bill thought to himself as he examined the receipts. He handed them back to Detective Cappiello saying, "I couldn't tell you if those are my signatures or not. I had been drinking all Wednesday night and continued on into Thursday."

"Where were the other places you went to on Wednesday?" Robbie said.

"I couldn't tell you. I was already pretty lit by the time we left the hotel."

"We see that a friend of McGuire sent a plane to Boca that same night to pick up some wine. You didn't happen to catch a ride back here did you?" Miller asked.

"Jim and Tommy got together and bought some wine. Tommy sent his jet down to get it and no, I wasn't on the plane. I'm sure you can check with the pilots or even watch the security video at the airports; I'm sure they have something set up."

"You have to admit that it's pretty coincidental, wouldn't you say," Miller said. Bill didn't answer. He was going to be as vague as possible with his answers without sounding like he was avoiding their questions or being deceitful. He didn't want to give them anything that they could use to trip him up later.

When it was obvious that Cunningham wasn't going to answer Miller's question, Robbie asked, "Tell me about Iraq. What did you do there?"

"I was a PSD. I ran around the country, letting people shoot at me while we tried to get our passengers to their meetings in one piece. I ran between the embassy, the airport and downtown Baghdad."

"Sounds a little hairy to me," Miller said.

"It was a lot of fun if you like that kind of excitement. The main route from the embassy to the airport is called Route Irish. You had to constantly check the side of the road for IED's or people on the roofs of the apartment buildings which lined the road. They would shoot at you every once in a while. Then there were the overpasses. You would have to approach them doing ninety to a hundred miles an hour, and then switch lanes just as you got to the overpass. The locals liked to drop mortars or hand grenades down on top of you. Like I said, it was a lot of fun."

"You get any specialized training to do that?" Robbie asked.

"Mostly relied on my SWAT training. I had to learn how to shoot an M-4 though. Never shot one before."

"No long range training with a rifle?" Miller asked.

"No. I was a trunk monkey. I sat in the back of our up armored Suburban with a SAW and kept cars away from the rear of our convoys."

"A saw? What's that? I wasn't in the military," Miller asked, looking a bit confused.

"Squad Automatic Weapon. A belt feed machine gun. Vehicles that didn't stay back behind the convoy got shot at if they came too close. You put the first rounds on the road in front of the car, if that didn't work, you aim at the front of the vehicle and if that didn't get their attention, you put a pattern through the windshield," Bill replied.

Miller was shocked. "You shot the drivers?"

"If they didn't stop when you put up the stop sign and they kept coming towards you, yes you lit them up."

"Have you talked to LaBrock since you got back?" Robbie asked.

"That slime ball. No. I don't ever want to have anything to do with him."

"Do you know anything about Maganelli's current business?"

"I can shorten this up a little. I haven't talked to John or Vince or anybody else connected with them since the law suit. I could care less what either one of them is doing now."

"Do you own a gun?" Miller asked.

"Yeah, my duty weapon from when I was a cop. A Smith and Wesson Model 19."

"Any rifles?"

"No. I'll make that easy for you too. I'll give you permission to search the house if you would like to."

Robbie was getting aggravated with Cunningham and he didn't care if it showed. The guy was insufferable and he knew that Cunningham was playing him. He was smart and had the same training that Robbie had, so now it was going to be a case of who slipped up first. Robbie's ace in the hole was LaBrock. No matter how tough he thought he was, he would want to talk to the detectives as soon as he got a real taste of the Broward County Jail. Robbie was guessing that LaBrock would have never been around the type of people he would now be thrown into a cell with. It was only going to be a matter of time before he would be asking, no make that begging to talk. Well, if Dietrich let him that is.

"We're going to get the shooter. I'll give LaBrock a few more days to think about going to jail for twenty years and then make him an offer. You were a cop. You want to bet that LaBrock doesn't roll over on his partners," Robbie said. He wanted to see what Cunningham's reaction would be to that question.

"I wish you the best of luck on that one. Now if you don't have any more questions, I think I've answered enough for one day."

Cappiello and Miller stood up and headed for the door. When they got to the door, Cappiello turned and said, "I'm going to get him to flip on someone. Don't be surprised if I'm not back here talking to you later." Bill didn't respond. He knew Detective Cappiello was baiting him and trying to get him to say something in his own defense. He just let the statement go and closed the door behind them.

When the detectives returned to the station there was a message from Dusty to call her. Robbie picked up the phone and dialed the

State's Attorney Office while Miller went to talk to Schultz about a Vegas road trip. Dusty had talked to Dietrich after the bond hearing and he wanted a meeting between his client and the detectives. Dusty wanted to know if they could be in her office the next morning. Robbie decided to call it a day and head for home for the night.

Early the following morning, Robbie and Miller met with Dusty a half hour before they were to meet with Dietrich. They went over what they had and came up with a strategy to deal with the situation. At the appointed time, they walked into a conference room where Dietrich and LaBrock were already seated. Miller looked at the pair and came to the conclusion that the total cost of the suits and watches Dietrich and LaBrock were wearing cost more than his car and he had a fairly nice car. Dusty, in typical fashion got right to the point.

"It's your meeting Kelly; does your client want to plead?"

"I'm not prepared to give you a check mark in the victory column just yet Dusty. My client does have some things that might be of interest to your detectives though."

"Let me guess. We drop the charges and your boy will tell us who did the shooting."

"Not quite, but he has some things for you to look at; then we will talk about dropping the charges."

"Let's hear it then."

"Mr. Maganelli borrowed money to help pay off some of the bills he had from Cunningham Fuel Injection," Dietrich said.

"You saying some bank president had him shot?" Dusty sarcastically asked.

"No! What I am saying is that Maganelli didn't go through normal channels to receive the funds he needed. He never told my client where he got the money, but it wasn't from their normal bank or from Mr. Maganelli's personal funds," Dietrich added.

"Could he have gone through some other commercial lender?" Dusty asked.

"No! Any loan application would have come through me to verify the company's financials," LaBrock said.

"This is a little convenient. Maganelli can't tell us anything because he's currently paralyzed and its unknown if he will ever recover and your client is telling us that he can provide an alternative suspect based on the testimony of something he says happened," Dusty said.

"It's possible that Maganelli borrowed some money from the wrong people. Mr. LaBrock can show that bills were being paid from an unknown source of income. It's something you need to look at because we plan to present this at trial," Dietrich said.

"Let me have my detectives check out this story and if we can find any independent proof of what your client is claiming, then we'll talk some more."

During the exchange between attorneys, Robbie was watching LaBrock and his body language. He was obviously nervous over the situation he found himself in, but nothing he did made Robbie think that what the lawyer was saying had been fabricated. He had to agree with Dusty, it seemed mighty convenient that this was coming to light after he had been arrested. He didn't seem to think it was important during any of their other talks. He would do his due diligence and try to check out LaBrock's story, but he wasn't buying it either.

The trio went back to Dusty's office after the meeting.

"You believe him?" Dusty asked Robbie.

"No, but I guess he could have found a loan shark to advance him some money. They generally don't take out the person who is repaying the loan though. They send a message by breaking legs or taking out someone else who is close enough to the person who took the loan so they are sure to get the message."

"McGuire was part of the businesses when this was supposed to have occurred; right? Do we have anything on McGuire?" Dusty said.

"No. The guy is clean as far as we can tell. He did send the jet here the day Maganelli was shot, but we checked on it. Customs did have a jet come in from Chile that same day. The paperwork shows they declared a shipment of wine on board. It looks like it was just a coincidence," Miller said.

"Your report showed these guys spent a lot of time in Vegas. No better place to find a loan shark and if McGuire spent a lot of time there, he might know someone," Dusty said.

"We're already planning to send Miller and Schultz to Vegas," Robbie said.

"Ok. Let's check out local loan sharks here and in Vegas; also McGuire, just so we can say we did and they can't use the alternative suspect as a defense," Dusty added.

Robbie then handed over the search warrant paperwork he had promised. Dusty quickly glanced it over and then placed the paperwork in a file folder she had in her briefcase. She thanked the pair for coming downtown and grabbed her briefcase. She followed them out the door to go to yet another meeting with a defense attorney. Miller and Cappiello discussed how they might check out LaBrock's story and decided that they needed to add Los Angeles to Miller's itinerary.

CHAPTER 23

Bill Cunningham had been a good cop and he was smart. Smart enough to know when to back off and reevaluate his actions. He realized after his last talk with Cappiello that he was becoming a little too confident and even arrogant. Cappiello was smart too and had Bill been honest with himself, he would have had to admit that the detective knew more than Bill did when it came to solving homicides. Bill decided that he should go and talk to Nicky and review the plan to once again make sure everything had gone according to the way he had set it up.

Nicky and Bill had continued with their normal routines when it came to their friendship and their families. They still helped each other out with projects and their families routinely got together for cookouts. They never once made mention of anything they had done while around their wives, except that first cookout after the shooting. Ginger, Nicky's wife had asked if Bill and Laura had heard about the shooting and didn't hold back anything when she gave her opinion on where Vince was going if everyone was lucky enough to have him pass on into the next world.

When Bill showed up at Nicky's the day after his conversation with Detective Cappiello, he found that Nicky was still a little shaken from his interview with the detective.

"Man, I think I screwed up when I talked to those detectives. I was really nervous and I know they noticed," Nicky said as the two of them sat down to talk in his kitchen. Ginger had gone off to shop, so they were free to talk and instead of going over the details of the plan, Bill found himself putting Nicky at ease.

"I told you that would happen and not to worry. It's a normal reaction. If they thought they had anything on you at all they would have invited you down to the station where they had more control and it would have been a lot more intimidating."

"I hope you're right. I don't want to talk to them anymore."

Bill had gotten up, grabbed a Coke from the refrigerator and said as he walked back to the table, "I had another talk with the detectives too and I can tell from their attitudes they want to nail me, but they still have nothing concrete to go on. They think they can get LaBrock to cut a deal and name me as his partner in this. He contacted Kelly Dietrich and I know this guy. He won't let LaBrock talk to the detectives."

"Are you sure that there is nothing to link him with you," Nicky asked as he sat nervously twisting a plastic drinking straw that had been left on the table. Bill watched this nervous reaction to the stress Nicky was feeling right then and knew he had to make sure Nicky was good with his side of the story.

"The phone got planted in his office as planned. I made sure that any prints on the phone were wiped clean when I put it into the bag and LaBrock doesn't know anything about that phone or how it got into his office."

"LaBrock has to know he's being set up. Will the police be able to connect the two of you in some way?"

"Even if he says something, he'll have no physical proof of anything that went on to back up his statements and there's no way he knows who the shooter was. The only way the police might learn something that would connect me in any way to this is if they find something in Vegas."

"Are you sure you covered your tracks out there?" Nicky inquired as he managed to break the straw in half.

"Kenny got to Vegas without being seen. I left the hotel in a cab and had it drop me at a location where we already knew there weren't any cameras and I then rode to the airport in a limo Jim had arranged. That airport gets a hundred limos a day, so no one is going to think twice about one pulling into a hanger. Even if they find out about the limo, Jim's story is that he sent it over to get the wine he ordered and it showed up at the wrong time."

"Did Kenny leave in the same limo?'

"Yeah. We switched clothes in the hanger and Kenny rode the limo back to the same spot where I was dropped off by the cab. He then got a cab and went back to the hotel. I got into the plane and the pilots didn't even bother to look back to see who their passenger was."

"Are you sure about the cameras at the hotel?"

"Nicky, we have been over this a bunch of times. Jim talked with a company who does the software for the same type of facial recognition program the hotels use. If they don't have a front facial shot, there is little they can use for comparison. When I got back to Vegas we just did the whole thing in reverse. Jim and Ken had a good time running up a bill on my credit card and both places they went to are really dark, so even if they show everyone there a picture from the hotel surveillance video, no one could say for certain that it wasn't me. Besides, they see a hundred new faces in those places every night. A barmaid isn't going to remember two guys having a few beers four weeks ago."

Nicky sat for a moment thinking over what Bill had just said, but he was still worried about his conversation with the police. "They really pissed off my boss when they showed up at work. He wanted to know why the cops wanted to talk to me. Do you think they will come and talk to me again?"

"No, I don't think they will. If they do, just remember to tell the truth and not give them too much information. People trip themselves up by running their mouths."

Nicky was much calmer after his talk with Bill who knew that the detectives wouldn't be talking to Nicky anymore, unless something unforeseen happened. Bill would soon find out if his deception had worked as planned. While he was in Nicky's kitchen, Miller and Schultz were eating dinner in their economy class seats on a plane bound for Vegas. They had an appointment with a Las Vegas detective in the morning who was going to help show them around. Their first stop would be the Mirage Hotel.

In the morning, the pair grabbed a cab and went to the Las Vegas Metropolitan Police Department where they met Detective Mike Key. Miller and Key had been to a narcotics conference together a few years back and had kept in touch. It would make it much easier to have a local detective with them as they tried to get information out of people who lived in a town which is known for keeping secrets.

The first thing the pair noticed when they walked into the hotel lobby was that the Mirage Hotel was a little nicer than the hotel the City of Plantation had put them in. As a matter of fact, you could have put their entire hotel inside the lobby of the Mirage. Neither had been to Vegas before and they had to force themselves to remember why they were there. Mike talked to a security guard who led them down a private hallway and into a very nice and expensively decorated office.

"This office belongs to a buddy of mine. He's their chief of security. He was my training officer until the hotel made him a much better deal than the city could," Mike said as he motioned for the two to sit down.

After a few minutes, a man dressed in a Hawaiian shirt and khaki pants walked in. He was roughly the size of a Mack truck and Miller noted the man had the largest hands he had ever seen as the man reached out to shake his hand. As he did, the man introduced himself as Skip Evens, the security director at the hotel. After a few comments by Key about Skip's attire, the four sat down to discuss why the Plantation detectives were in sin city. After explaining what they wanted to see at the Mirage, Schultz asked Skip about the loan sharks in the city and told him about LaBrock's alternative theory.

"After we check our records and we look at the videos you want to review, I'll make a couple of calls and see what I can dig up. Since I left the department, I've made some questionable acquaintances who might be able to help" Skip stated.

"I don't want to know anything about that part of it so I can claim plausible deniability if I'm called before Internal Affairs," Key said with a laugh.

"Don't worry. I always covered your ass while I was on the department, so one more time won't matter."

Skip stood up and motioned for them to follow. He led the group down several stark white hallways and through several security doors which would have rivaled anything the Pentagon had. They finally ended up in a room lined with rows of operators, monitoring a wall covered with closed circuit television screens. Some operators were intently watching players and dealers as cards and chips moved across the dealer's tables while others watched slot machines and poker tables. When an operator spotted something unusual, he manipulated the computer key board and mouse to zoom the camera in as close to the action as he needed to; making sure that the activity he was watching was legal or at least tolerated by the hotel.

Skip walked over and sat down at a computer desk and began typing. He asked the names of the people the detectives were interested in and the dates of their stay. After finding the proper records, he then programmed the computer to display the rooms that McGuire and Cunningham had stayed in. After a bit more typing, Skip was able to display the two rooms in question on the monitors and keyed up the video to match up with the computers record of when each hotel room door was opened. Miller had obtained the driver's license pictures of both McGuire and Cunningham and handed them to Skip for comparison.

After watching the monitors for several minutes, Skip said, "I've got a good facial shot of McGuire, but the other guy, Cunningham is wearing a hoodie which covers his face up enough so that I can't use it for a facial recognition comparison."

"Can you check other parts of the hotel or casino to see if you get a better shot," Schultz asked.

"I'll run McGuire and have the computer track him. If they're together, maybe we'll get lucky and get a good face shot."

Skip typed away and brought up several more video clips of McGuire and Cunningham leaving or entering the hotel, but each shot showed Cunningham's face covered by the hoodie or looking down as he walked. Surprisingly, there were no shots of the two on the casino floor which even the two detectives from Florida, who knew nothing of what was "normal" for gamblers in Vegas, found odd. Yes, it was possible that they gambled at other casinos, but not very likely that they excluded the casino at their own hotel. Skip printed out the door opening log for the rooms the pair stayed in and rechecked the hotel's records for any credit card activity, but did not come up with anything different from what the detectives already had. He also made some notes on a piece of paper with the times from the videos of when the pair left the hotel and handed it to Miller. The group then left the monitoring area and returned to Skip's office.

"In the five years I've been here, I've never seen someone who stayed in our hotel not drop at least one quarter into one of our slots," Skip said as he sat back down at his desk.

"I'll take this list of exit times and see if we can compare it to the times they used their credit cards around town. Maybe there's something there?" Key said.

"Something else I find odd is that Cunningham has on the same hoodie each time he leaves the room. He's gone from the hotel all day, but when he returns he's got that hoodie on and it's still covering his face. It's almost like he knows about our camera system and how to get around it," Skip said.

"That's something we can use, but I'd like to see his face somewhere so I could positively say that yes, he was here. We think he's our shooter and what you've showed me so far still makes me think that he was somehow able to get out of town undetected," Miller said.

"Let's stop by the two places he used the credit cards and see if we get lucky. This is Vegas after all," Key said with a little laugh.

The trio stood up to leave Skip's office and as they did, Skip told them that he would make the phone calls he had promised earlier to see if Maganelli had been borrowing money from anyone in town. He said that it would take a little while, but that he would have something for them before they left town. Miller promised Skip a seafood dinner if he ever came to South Florida, thanked him for his help and the three then headed out of the hotel and left in Key's car.

Key pulled out onto South Las Vegas Boulevard and headed towards PT's Bar. He had already called ahead and found out from the manager that the barmaid who was listed on the credit card receipt was working that day.

The three were met by the hostess as they walked into the sports bar. Mike asked to speak to Tony who was the manager and after a brief conversation the trio was escorted to a booth located at the rear of the bar. Tony left after they were seated and a couple of minutes passed before a tall blond walked up and introduced herself.

"Hi, I'm Barb. Tony said you wanted to talk to me about a credit card receipt."

"Yeah, that's right. I'm Detective Key of the Las Vegas Police Department and these are Detectives Miller and Schultz from the Plantation P.D. in Plantation, Fl. We just wanted to see if you remember a couple of guys who were in here last month."

"Last month? I have a hard time remembering who was in here yesterday. We get a lot of tourists in here and except for the jerks who hit on me, I really don't pay much attention, but I'll try."

Miller was admiring Barb as she spoke to them. She was tall, shapely and had a killer smile. He knew little of Vegas, but guessed she would have made a perfect showgirl. Barb caught Miller checking her out and gave him a smile, asking him how long he was going to be in town. Miller would have normally followed up that comment with small talk and an offer to meet later, but he knew his time was limited and he didn't want an audience if was going to put his moves on some cute girl.

"Unfortunately we're only here for a day or two. We have this important case we're on and our boss wants this finished up as soon as possible."

Miller opened a folder he was carrying and pulled out copies of the credit card receipt and pictures of McGuire and Cunningham which he had gotten from their driver licenses. He then handed them over to Barb. She examined the copies and looked back at Miller.

"That's my code on the receipt, but I don't remember seeing either one of them in here."

"I know this was a while ago, but please take another look. This is a shooting where the victim might die and we are trying to find out if these guys were in here as they claimed," Miller emphasized.

Barb took a longer look at both pictures, but was still unable to remember whether either had ever been her customers. She handed Miller back his copies and apologized for her inability to be of assistance. He placed the copies back in the folder.

"Maybe if they had hit on you we might have gotten lucky," Miller joked.

"I even tend to forget about those jerks after a couple of days. Since you're already here, can I get you some menus? We have a couple of really good specials today."

"Sounds good!" Schultz said as he realized that his stomach was still on east coast time and he was really hungry. The other two agreed and Barb left to get the menus, but not before giving Miller a sly little smile as she left.

"Too bad you're out of here tomorrow. That could be promising," Key said as he smiled at Miller. Barb returned and after some small talk about what it was like to live in South Florida, she took their orders and went off to take care of her other customers. Over lunch, the three talked about the possible scenarios which would explain why they hadn't seen Cunningham's face in any of the videos they had watched. Key pointed out that Cunningham's actions at the hotel were unusual, but he'd learned over the years that what was normal for other places just didn't happen in his town.

Miller was still convinced that Cunningham was the shooter and that he somehow slipped out of town. McGuire arranged for the plane to fly to South Florida and Cunningham might have been onboard. The man in the hoodie could have been a double. Miller pulled out the picture of Cunningham and mentally pictured Martin. The two were about the same size and had similar looking faces. It would not have been hard for Martin to have somehow caught a ride to Vegas from one of his pilot buddies. Miller had talked to Martin's neighbors and two had remembered Martin's Monte Carlo in his driveway. They however, couldn't say for sure that they remembered actually seeing Martin during the time of the shooting. Key added that the airport had a lot of video cameras covering most of the hangers. If Cunningham had left or Martin had come in on a private plane they might get lucky and have him on video. This was after all, Vegas.

The manager had offered to comp the three for their lunch, but they decided that it would be better to pay than have someone make a complaint later. Miller managed to slip Barb his business card on his way out of the bar. He had put his cell phone number on it and made the comment as he handed it to her that she should get in touch with him if she ever came to Florida. Schultz watched this transaction and chuckled to himself as he held the door open for Miller. The two exchanged glances as Miller passed Schultz.

"Shut up!" Miller said as he gave Schultz's side a friendly jab with his elbow as he passed.

The three then headed off to Steiner's before going out to the airport. They left Steiner's without any more information than what they already had when they walked in. No one remembered the middle aged, grey haired man accompanied by the guy in a hoodie. Yes, the credit card was used there, but this was also a popular bar with tourists and no one working that night remembered ever seeing either McGuire or Cunningham.

Key turned off the main road and onto an access road which led to a group of businesses located on the west side of the airport. He parked in the lot of the air charter service who leased the hanger used by Anderson Investment. Key had already checked and luckily they still had the surveillance video for the week in question. The office manager handed Detective Key five video cassettes and offered them an office where they could view the videos. There were four days of video on these cassettes and they needed a plan if there was any hope of getting through them in a reasonable amount of time. Miller pulled out a pad of paper and wrote down the times he believed Cunningham would have been at the airport. This was based on the information he already had from the flight plan of Anderson Investment's jet which he'd received from the FAA.

"Fast forward the tape to 7pm Wednesday night. The plane leaves the airport at 7:30 and I'm sure Cunningham didn't want to hang around here and possibly get seen by someone," Miller said to Key who obliged by pressing the fast forward on the remote control he was holding. He hit the "play" button when a black Cadillac limousine was seen pulling up on the tarmac in front of the hanger. They watched the video as the car waited for the hanger doors to open. The car then pulled into the hanger and the doors were shut behind it. They watched for a few more minutes and saw the hanger doors open a second time. The car exited first, followed by the jet being towed from the hanger.

"Well that was useless," Schultz said.

"The video is too dark to get a tag number off the limo, but the numbers on the tail of the jet matched the one listed on the flight plan," Miller replied.

"Let's see what we have when it comes back," Key said.

Miller looked at his notes and said, "Fast forward to about 5pm Thursday."

At 5:32pm a black limo was seen entering the hanger, but once again the area proved too dark for the car's tag number to be seen on the video. A little after 6pm, the scene they had seen before was repeated. The jet was towed into the hanger directly after it landed and the car was seen exiting the hanger a few minutes later. After viewing the video several times, they were still unable to obtain any information on the car's tags or who the passengers might be.

It was getting late and Key wanted to get back to the station to check up on a couple of cases which were coming up for trial. He dropped Schultz and Miller off at their hotel and told them he would be back in the morning to pick them up. Miller decided that the first thing he needed to do once he got back to his room was call Cappiello and give him an update.

"I thought those casinos had really sophisticated software which could follow anyone, anywhere," was Robbie's response after listening to Miller's description of the day's events.

"They're good, but they need at least a partial view of the face to work," Miller replied.

"Did it look like he was hiding his face on purpose?"

"It's hard to say, but the security guy at the hotel said that it wasn't normal behavior. I also think that it would be a good idea to have someone go over to the Boca airport and see what they have on video if you already haven't done that. See if they can see anyone getting out of the plane besides the pilots."

There were a few moments of silence on the phone while Cappiello tried to decide what his next move was going to be. He would be able to explain at trial that Cunningham's actions were suspicious, but an attorney would have a hundred explanations as to why he acted as he did in the hotel. Based on what Miller had told him, he was even surer now that Cunningham had flown back to Florida. Robbie shook his head in silence as he thought to himself that he still didn't have the proof he needed to lock up that arrogant asshole. He told Miller to follow up with Evens on the loan shark angle and if nothing came of that, head out to Los Angeles to talk to McGuire. After he hung up the phone, Miller started going over the notes he had made throughout the day. A few minutes went by when he was distracted by an advertisement which was playing on the television for the monthly special at the Golden Nugget Casino. He picked up the phone and called Shultz's room.

"You had enough work for one day?" Miller asked.

"I've already changed into my lucky shirt," Schultz replied.

"Meet you in the lobby in ten."

Key's call woke up Miller the next morning. Key said that Skip had some information and that he would pick up Miller and Schultz out in front of their hotel in an hour. Key was right on time and gave out a laugh as Miller sat in the car seat next to him. He then glanced over his shoulder as Schultz sat down in the rear passenger seat.

"Where did you two go last night and what time did you get in?" Key asked.

"We hit a few places and ended up at PT's and before you ask, no she wasn't working," Miller chuckled.

Key could only laugh as he turned out onto the highway to go back to the Mirage. Once they arrived, the three were led back to Skip's office where he was waiting for them. He was once again in a Hawaiian shirt and Miller wondered what the dress code was for employees of the hotel. Skip looked over at Miller and realized that he was looking at his shirt.

"I can wear anything I want and I like these shirts."

"Sorry. Just not use to the life style in Vegas," Miller said.

Skip didn't take offense and picked up a notebook from his desk. He had made the calls he promised to make. While he waited for Skip to share this new information, Miller began wondering who Skip had called and how he would have met them in the first place. Miller had met some questionable people while working vice and even had one or two help him with some information on a case, but not to this extent. Skip must be really trusted by the people he talked to. This was not the type of information people who wanted to stay out of jail usually shared with others.

"I really don't have anything for you which, in the long run could be a good thing," Skip said.

"Were you able to talk to the people you told us about yesterday?" Schultz asked.

"Yeah. I called a couple of guys who fund the bigger loans and they said that no one has approached them about floating a loan for your victim. I know these guys. If they don't know about it then it didn't happen here."

"Do they have any connections in South Florida?" Miller asked.

"I figured that would be your next question and they do, but said there was nothing on the streets about your guy getting any large loans down there either."

Miller realized that he had hit another dead end, so he stood up and reached out to shake Skip's hand. He thanked him for his help, reminded Skip about the dinner offer if he ever came south and left the office followed by the other two. Miller avoided the temptation to drop some change into the slot machines on the way out of the hotel. Once outside, the three stood outside Key's car and discussed what was going to happen next. Just then, Miller's cell phone rang. It was Robbie with what might be their last glimmer of hope. Tommy Barnes from Anderson Investment had called Robbie and told him that his pilot was out at the airport and would talk to them if they could get there before noon.

It took about twenty minutes for them to get to the airport. Key pulled his car onto the tarmac in front of the hanger leased by Anderson Investment. The hanger doors were open and they saw a man inside the hanger examining the front wheels of what they all imagined was a very expensive private jet. The man stood up as they approached and introduced himself as Frank LaCoda.

"You the cops from Florida? Mr. Barnes said you might be stopping by."

"We understand that you took a trip down to Boca Raton to pick up some wine for Mr. Barnes a few weeks ago," Miller said.

"That's right. Flew down and picked up the wine, then headed back as soon as it was loaded. Is there some problem with the wine? It was cleared by customs when the other plane brought it up from Chile."

"No, it's not the wine we're interested in. Did you have anyone onboard with you during the flight to Boca or back to Vegas?" Schultz asked.

"Just Bob, the co-pilot," was LaCota's response.

Miller leaned in closer to LaCota. "You sure? We're investigating a shooting that might turn into a homicide. If we find out that you're not telling the truth, you could be charged as an accessory."

LaCota stood his ground and was not backing down from Miller. "I don't like to be threatened. I told you there were two of us and some wine. Check the video at the airports. There are enough cameras around here."

Schultz then stepped in and got uncomfortably close to LaCota. "Wants' Bob's last name?" he said as he squared off with LaCota.

"You two can play the tough cop bit somewhere else. I'm retired from LAPD and that shit is not going to work on me. Now both of you back off and get out of my hanger."

Miller looked at Schultz and the two both took a step back. They were out of their jurisdiction and didn't want to get into a fight or get Key involved with doing any paperwork. "You didn't give us Bob's last name," Miller said.

LaCota had not relaxed his posture and his attitude had also remained the same. "You're right and I'm not giving you anything more. It's on my flight plan and now it's time for you all to leave."

Key motioned for Schultz and Miller to follow and all three left the hanger to return to the car. Once in the car, Miller made a note to call Robbie and get the co-pilot's name off of his copy of the flight plan he had on his desk at the station. Key took them back to the hotel where they decided to relax for the rest of the day before heading out to

Los Angeles the next morning. Key passed on Miller's offer for dinner saying that he had to prepare for a trial he was subpoenaed for in the morning. As he prepared to leave, Key made mention of the condition he had found them in when he had picked them up and advised that maybe they should take it a little easier if they wanted to catch the early flight in the morning. Miller and Schultz took Key's advice and made it to the airport first thing in the morning.

CHAPTER 24

The pair did little talking on the flight from Vegas to Los Angeles mostly due to their hangovers. They grabbed a rental car and were headed out towards Santa Monica and their morning appointment with Mr. Barnes.

"How do you want to approach this guy?" Schultz asked.

"Let's just keep it low profile. See where the conversation takes us. I want to see if he contradicts any of the information we already have."

"I think he said something to that pilot about keeping his mouth shut. I wonder where an ex-cop gets the money and experience to be flying private jets," Schultz said.

"I know one the of the Ft. Lauderdale PD aviation guys. The city pays for their training, and then they pick up flying jobs on the side. They just keep moving up into bigger planes. That guy said he was with LAPD and they have a huge aviation unit."

"He was an ass. I wonder how he and Barnes met and how he became his pilot?"

"I guess we'll have to ask Barnes," Miller said as he pulled into the office building parking lot where Anderson Investment was located.

They didn't have to wait in the lobby very long before a secretary led them into an ornately furnished conference room. The room was filled with old artifacts and paintings, mostly from Africa. The pair was examining what appeared to be a tribal headdress which was housed inside a glass case when a high pitched voice spoke from behind them.

"That one is really rare. It's from the Sua tribe in Central Africa. The Sua's are one of three groups of pygmies, collectively called the

BaMbuti, of the Ituri Rainforest. That one is estimated to be about two hundred years old," the voice said. Miller and Schultz turned and were a little taken back when they saw the source of the almost feminine voice. Standing before them was a black man who was about six foot tall and every bit of two hundred and fifty pounds, but showed no sign of any body fat. His graying hair put him in his sixties, but his physical appearance would have put him much younger. Miller reached out to shake the now extended hand and noticed a large, diamond studded ring on the man's pinky finger.

"Tom Barnes. Nice to meet you. Do either of you want something to drink?" the man said.

"No we're good. I'm Detective Miller and this is Detective Schultz."

"Please take a seat. As you might have figured, I deal in African art, mostly antique tribal collections," Barnes said as he pointed towards the conference table.

"We don't want to take up much of your time. We just have to follow up on the leads we have developed in a shooting case we are working," Miller said as he and Schultz sat down.

"No problem. Today is a slow day so ask whatever you want."

"I have to ask. Is that a Super Bowl ring?" Miller asked as he looked at the ring on Barnes' finger.

"That's what it is. I got it in my rookie year with the Rams. Mostly sat on the bench that year then got traded to the Oilers the following year. Ended up as a blocking back for Earl Campbell, but a knee injury put me out of the game."

"You played with Earl Campbell! I guess he owes some of his fame to you then," Schultz said as he now studied the ring on Barnes' hand.

"I guess you could say that. He's all crippled up now, but I'm still in pretty good shape for a guy my age."

Miller decided to get past the present line of questioning and get down to why they were there. Barnes was very relaxed and not the least bit nervous over the fact that two cops were now going to be questioning him. Miller pulled out his notebook, reviewed a couple of pages and looked back towards Barnes.

"I have a couple of questions about the plane you sent to Florida back on October 20th. I understand that you sent it down to pick up some wine."

"A friend of mine from here in the building had a chance to invest in some wine from Chile."

Schultz looked puzzled. "Invest? What do you mean by invest? Do you mean like investing in stocks?"

"That's exactly what I mean. You can buy up wine that promises to be a good year, sit on it while it ages and then it goes up in value. Sometimes, if you're lucky it goes up a lot."

"Why send a private jet? That has to be a lot more expensive than having a commercial carrier ship it to you?" Miller asked.

"You're right about that, but I can be sure it arrives safely and unbroken if the wine is on my plane."

"Makes sense. Did you allow any passengers on the trip?"

"No. I talked to Frank right after you left the hanger yesterday and he said you asked about that. I guess he was a little abrupt with you two."

Schultz spoke up before Miller could answer. "We might have come on a little strong with him. We apologize for that."

"I hired Frank when he retired from LAPD. I go into some places on business which are not all that nice and it made sense to have someone who could take care of not only themselves, but also me. He's not the most personable person on the planet, but that's not what I pay him for."

"Would he have taken a passenger without you knowing about it?" Miller asked.

"I'm not saying that it didn't happen, but Frank is loyal and truthful. He told me it was just him and the co-pilot and that's good enough for me." Miller watched Barnes' body language and listened to his voice as he spoke and decided that Barnes believed what he was saying. He then moved on to questions about McGuire.

"I understand that Mr. McGuire was your partner in this investment. How long have you two known each other?"

"I moved my business into this building about eight years ago. That's when I met Jim. We became friends and when one of us hears of an investment opportunity, we ask the other if they want in. Jim was the one who found this deal and made all of the arrangements. After I checked it out, I decided to purchase fifty percent of the wine from him."

"McGuire found the deal?" Schultz questioned as he began flipping through his notebook. "When we talked a couple of weeks ago you said that you had bought the wine." Both detectives then waited to see if this little inconsistency might lead to something. Sometimes a simple slip up like this one can begin to unravel a well prepared and rehearsed story, but Barnes had no reaction. He just said it was a slip of the tongue and continued explaining the details of the deal he made with McGuire.

Miller realized that either Barnes was very well briefed or he was actually telling the truth. Either way, he didn't see that he would get any more information than he already had from Barnes, so he decided to end the meeting. The detectives stood up, thanked Barnes for his time and made their way to McGuire's office for their next scheduled appointment.

McGuire's office was not as palatial as Barnes' had been, but it still showed that the owner had made his mark in the business world. The walls were covered in mahogany paneling and the chairs were all covered with brown leather. There was an oil painting of a fox hunt and one of what appeared to be a European style farm. The office could have been mistaken for a sitting room in an English manor house. The detectives were asked to wait while Mr. McGuire completed a phone call and after a few minutes he appeared, apologizing for the delay. He then led the pair down a hallway. As they walked down the hallway, Miller was looking at the framed photographs which lined the walls. He saw pictures of McGuire with people who he recognized as actors and even one of McGuire and President Gerald Ford. He took special notice of one picture in particular. Miller stopped to take a closer look at it.

"Is this one of you and Bill Cunningham?" Miller asked McGuire.

McGuire stopped and returned to the photo Miller was pointing to.

"Yes, that's Bill and the other guy is his brother, David."

"You have pictures of a lot of famous people on this wall. How do they rate such a spot?"

"They were my business partners and even more important, they're my friends or at least Bill is now since Dave has passed away." McGuire turned without saying any more and walked into an office at the end of the hall. The detectives followed as Jim closed the door behind them. Miller and Schultz sat down in chairs which were in front of Jim's desk and noticed that the office had the same look and feel as the lobby; very formal, yet comfortable.

Miller started the conversation by saying, "Thanks for seeing us on such short notice. We're trying to fill in some gaps in the information we have on the Maganelli shooting and we're hoping you might be able to help."

"I figured you would be checking into Vince's past. I just didn't figure that you would come all this way to talk to me in person."

"We have to check out all the information we're given and there were too many questions we needed answered to do it over the phone," Schultz said.

"I'm sure you have already talked to people back in South Florida about my involvement with Vince's companies and how he screwed me over. You asked me when you called on the phone about my involvement with Cunningham Fuel Injection and I told you pretty much everything I know, so what else do you need to know?"

Miller decided that he needed to be very careful as to how he worded his questions. He did not want to scare McGuire to the point that he stopped answering his questions, but he needed to see if he could find an inconsistency in his story which might make him slip up and implicate either himself or Cunningham.

"Our biggest question is about the plane which you arranged to go to Florida the morning Mr. Maganelli was shot," Miller said.

"I have nothing to hide. I was on the phone with Tom while you were in the lobby and he told me about the questions you asked him during your meeting. He and I do a lot of deals together and this one was set up months before Vince was shot. It was just coincidence that Tom's plane was in Florida that morning."

Miller studied McGuire as he spoke, looking for any signs that he was being untruthful. He was not as good at doing this as Cappiello was, but he knew enough to know when he was being lied to. McGuire was hard to read. He looked his age which Miller knew from his research was sixty three. He had short grey hair and a slight Georgia accent which Miller was sure had softened during his years of living in California. He looked every bit the part of a guy who had made his living working with computers.

"But while the plane was on its way to Florida, you and Cunningham were partying in Vegas?" Schultz asked.

"Is that a question or a statement? Bill and I go to Vegas a couple times a year. We have ever since we started going there when we had our company. This trip was planned just after Bill came back from Iraq. A long time before Vince was shot."

Miller continued watching and noticed that McGuire was becoming a little uneasy and that he had trouble keeping eye contact. He decided to ask a couple of pointed questions to see what reaction he got.

"I find it strange that after Vince was shot, Bill didn't call. We checked the phone records and you two have not talked since before the shooting. Seems to me that the two of you would have been talking a lot, if for no other reason than to gloat over Maganelli's misfortune."

"I don't know what your records show, but I did talk to Bill as soon as he got back to Florida. He called me as soon as he heard the news. I assumed that he called me from home, but you're right about not talking to him after that. I've been traveling on business."

Miller did not get the reaction he was hoping for. McGuire was still a little uneasy and shifted his weight in his chair as he spoke, but he didn't miss a beat with his answers. He tried to decide if McGuire was well schooled in his answers or whether he was relaying the events as they actually happened. Miller decided to ask just a few more questions to see where they would lead him.

"Tell me about your stay in Vegas."

"What's to tell? We stayed at the Mirage, but don't like the tables at the big casinos, so we spent our time at a couple of the ones off the strip. We had too much to drink and eat and generally had a good time. What else is there in Vegas?"

"We saw the video at the hotel of you and Cunningham. Any reason he kept his face down and covered? He had a hoodie pulled up over his head the whole time he was in the hotel. It almost looks like he was trying not to be seen by their security cameras."

"Couldn't tell you. I know the bright lights bother him and the hotel was really cold. He just came back from a country where the temperatures were well over a hundred degrees all the time. I'm sure that was part of it."

"Did you rent any limos during the time you and Cunningham were in Vegas?" Shultz asked.

"Yeah I did, but I didn't ride in them. I sent one over to the airport to pick up the wine when the plane came in."

Schultz had been bothered by one item involving the wine. He had also picked up on McGuire's increasing uneasiness and decided it was a good time to get an answer. "Why did the wine end up in Vegas if you and Barnes live here."

"Tom has a home in Vegas and we intend to sell the wine to the upscale restaurants on the strip."

"We viewed the footage from the airport and saw that a limo showed up to Anderson Investment's hanger twice. Once when the plane left and again when it returned. Did you and Cunningham jump on the plane for the ride down to Florida? If it was me, I would have at least wanted to see if my investment was safe and loaded onto the plane properly," Schultz said.

"Well you're not me. I don't remember exactly where we were, but I know there are a couple of credit card receipts floating around somewhere which places both of us in Vegas when Vince was shot. I pay my people well to look after my investments and I can't answer why the limo showed up twice, but I can tell you Bill and I were not in it. Now, unless you have any other questions, I need to get back to work."

That was the reaction Miller was looking for. They had touched a nerve. Now what does he do to exploit it? He had answered their questions, but had not given them anything new and he had reasonable explanations for all of their questions. They were now getting thrown out of his office, but he needed to take one more shot.

"Just one more thing before we go. No plan is perfect. We'll find a mistake somewhere and when we do, someone is going to jail. I don't think you're telling me everything and I'm going to find out what really happened. My guess is that you and Cunningham made a deal with LaBrock to get back what was owed to you and I'm going to make sure I find the evidence which proves that."

McGuire went to respond, but stopped himself before saying anything. Bill had actually grilled him during their meetings and had tried to trip him up with questions like the ones Miller was asking. The one thing he had learned was to know when to keep his mouth shut. Miller's statement was designed to get an emotional response and McGuire was not going to give him one; especially one that was not well thought out and could be used in the future to tear apart his story. He just pointed towards the door and asked once again for the detectives to leave.

Once he was sure they had left the building, Jim opened the safe in his office and went to grab the cell phone Bill had given him, but stopped himself from dialing it. He and Bill had set up times in which they would talk by phone and it was not yet the prescribed time. They had made this arrangement so they could be sure that they did not have the phones on them when being questioned or watched. If the police didn't know about the phones in the first place, they would have no way to trace the calls. Bill had made special arrangements to supply the key players with cell phones which could not be traced back to him or anyone else in the group. Jim just needed to remember to stick to the plan to make sure it had its intended ending.

CHAPTER 25

Jay Goldman had kept to his new routine, working some Thursdays over the past month instead of his usual weekend shifts. He still stopped in every morning at the restaurant and wondered if it was really for the food or the chance to talk to Barbara. She had smiled to herself when she saw him pull up and had made sure he was seated at one of her tables. They made some small talk while he ordered breakfast and she left to place his order.

Jay was engrossed in a newspaper article he was reading and was a little startled when someone walked up and sat in the chair across from him. He looked up to see Sam Bonner.

"Mind if I join you?" Bonner said as he grabbed a menu which was stacked in between the sugar dispenser and ketchup bottle on the end of the table.

"No, I don't mind. You starting early?" Jay asked as he wondered why the detective was out and about at 7am.

"Got court at nine and didn't have anything in the house to eat."

"I usually try to get a little extra sleep and eat after briefing," Jay replied.

"I wish I could get some extra sleep. I've been putting a lot of hours in on your buddy's shooting."

Jay was no longer curious as to why the detective was out so early. He had quickly developed a very uneasy feeling that it was not just a coincidence that Bonner had decided to eat in this restaurant after all. He knew he was about to be questioned about the shooting to see if he knew more than he was letting on. Luckily, Barbara ended Bonner's questioning by returning to the table to let Jay know that his order would be right up. She then turned and asked Bonner if he wanted anything. Jay was able to get himself composed as Bonner placed his order.

"I heard they sent Miller and Schultz out to Vegas. Must be nice to be a detective?" Jay said. Bonner didn't respond right away, but got right to the point of the real reason he had joined Jay for breakfast.

"I've got some questions which I'm hoping you can give me some answers to," Sam said.

"What would you like to know?"

"We've checked the phone records of everyone whose names have come up during the investigation including some of the people who knew him in the past. It's funny that none of these people called one another after the shooting."

"I take it that I'm one of those people?" Jay asked.

"We have a list of people who went to school with Maganelli and were in business with him later on. It seems to me that having one of your classmates shot would be a big deal, but it appears that no one made a call to even say, "Hey, did you hear the news?""

Jay had now gotten over his initial uneasiness and had regained his inner composure. He was ready for Bonner and his questions. Jay took a minute to answer because he wanted to make sure that his response didn't make Bonner think that he was pissed off by the question or that he was being less than truthful in his answer.

"Well for starters, I was the first patrolman on the scene and I know it's an active investigation. I'm sure the department would not be too happy about me talking with friends of mine about an active investigation."

Bonner was not expecting that answer, but had to agree with Jay that it was indeed the proper action for him to have taken. Bonner, however had been sent by Cappiello to "feel out" Officer Goldman to see what additional information he might have or maybe failed to inform the detectives about.

"I just found that unusual," Sam said.

"Well if it makes you feel better, I did talk to Bill Cunningham later that day. He lives in my zone."

"Have you talked to him since?"

"Yeah, we talk all the time, but usually in person when I'm working. We really haven't talked about Vince since the first couple of days after he was shot. Neither one of us likes him even though we were once his friends and personally, I could care less what happens to him."

Bonner was satisfied with Jay's answers and changed the subject. He then asked if Jay was going to the FOP picnic over the weekend. His assignment over, Bonner ate quickly, citing his need to get to court and left. Jay had not yet finished his meal when Barbara came over. She knew it was against the rules of the restaurant, but she sat down in the chair Bonner had just vacated.

"Problems?" she asked Jay.

"Work related."

"Did you know he was in here last week asking questions about you? Are you in some sort of trouble?"

"No, I'm ok. What type of questions was he asking?"

"He asked if I knew you very well and if I knew why you had changed your schedule. I told him you were a little burned out at your other job and needed a change."

"Thanks. That's basically what it is."

"Jay, I think you know I like you a lot, so if there is anything I can do for you…" Barbara left the rest unsaid, but accented her words by running her foot up the inside of Jay's leg. She wanted to make sure Jay knew that she would be willing to help out anyway she could. As a matter of fact, she was hoping that Jay felt the same way and would take her up on her obvious, unspoken offer.

Jay had not expected the sexual advance, but liked it just the same. He did like Barbara. He wondered what she would be like if he managed to get her into bed and after what just happened; it seemed like a sure thing. He then did something that he did not usually do while in uniform, he wrote down his phone number on a napkin and slid it across the table. Barbara quickly picked it up, looked around to see if her manager had spotted the restaurant's rules violation and stood up. She smiled at Jay and asked if it would be alright if she called him after she got off work.

Jay returned the smile and also stood up. He paid his bill and left the restaurant, but not before giving one last look at Barbara. He was pleased at what had just transpired between the two of them, but at the same time he was now concerned that Bonner was checking him out. He decided that he would make a stop by to talk with Cunningham later in the day.

Jay actually waited until after he got off shift before heading over to Cunningham's house. Bill had met him at the door and the two went out to the back patio and sat by the pool. Laura was home, but watching TV and decided not bother them.

"One of the detectives assigned to Vince's case has been asking questions about me," Jay said.

"What type of questions?"

"He wanted to know why no one made any calls to talk about Vince after he was shot," Jay replied.

"What did you say?" Bill asked.

Jay explained that he had told Bonner about his concerns with discussing an active investigation, but that the two of them had talked in person. He told Bill that he was unsure if Bonner had accepted the answer, but also mentioned that Bonner had been asking questions prior to today's meeting. Cunningham began to wonder if he had made a mistake by limiting the phone traffic amongst the group. If so, the question should be easily explained away. There was no love lost between anyone in the group and Vince, so why would any of them be overly concerned about his well being. Yet this one oversight could be the one thing that might trip up someone while being questioned by the police. He needed to give it some further thought.

Jay also told Bill about Barbara's advances. This actually concerned Bill more than Bonner poking around. Men have a tendency to tell girlfriends things which need to go unsaid. There was not only jail time, but a lot of money riding on the outcome of his plan. He didn't believe Jay would be the type of person who would try and impress a girl with a story of how he and his friends had outsmarted the police and had gotten away with a crime. He didn't pursue the issue.

"Jay, I wouldn't worry about Bonner. I think you gave him a good answer and I will make sure the others tell the same story if they get questioned. Just make sure you keep this to yourself and keep the girl in the dark."

Jay was a little aggravated that Bill would think he would mention anything about this case to Barbara. He had committed several crimes himself during this conspiracy to make sure everything went as planned. He wasn't going to mention anything to anyone. If for no other reason than cops don't fare very well in prison. He assured Bill that he had no intention of letting Barbara in on the plan, but worried about the others if questioned. Bill assured him that he would talk with the others and that it was not something that would unravel the plan. At least that is what he was secretly hoping, but he was not going to reveal his concerns to Jay. About this time, Laura came out to the patio to ask if Jay wanted to stay for dinner. He declined saying that he needed to get home and left.

"What was that about?" Laura asked sensing that Jay was uneasy about something.

"Jay got hit on by a waitress and wanted to know if it was a good idea to take her out," Bill said as he motioned for his wife to sit on his lap.

"Really? A waitress or some stripper he met at one of those clubs?"

"OK, a stripper, but don't tell him I told you so."

Laura took up Bill's invitation and sat down. As she did, she put her one arm around Bill's neck, and then reached across his body to grab his hand. She snuggled in as close as she could get to her husband, pushing herself up tight against him. The two sat quietly for a few moments. They were both staring at the bright blue waters of their swimming pool, lost in their own thoughts until the yelling of children a couple of houses over broke the silence. Laura turned towards Bill's face and looked deeply into his eyes. "You're not telling me something," she said.

CHAPTER 26

Bonner walked into the station's detective bureau and pulled a chair over to Cappiello's desk. He sat down and waited for Robbie to finish reading a report he had in his hand before talking to him about the case. He had followed up on the couple of things Robbie asked him to do and wanted to fill Cappiello in on the details. When Cappiello finished reading the report, he looked up at Sam.

"Did you find out anything?" Robbie asked.

"Not a great deal. Nothing we can really use."

"What about the airport surveillance cameras?" Robbie said as he finally put the report he was reading back into its folder. He waited for the answer as he looked at the pile of reports on his desk which was not getting any smaller even though his time with the department was running out.

"Nothing of any use. It's too dark to see if anyone gets out of the plane when it arrives, but you can see a set of headlights from a car as it leaves the back of the hanger shortly after the plane arrives. Then at about 2:55 p.m., a car pulls up and parks in the lot, but the camera only catches the front corner of the car. Someone gets out of the passenger side and walks around the side of the car then enters the hanger through a side door, but I can't make a positive ID on who it was. A few minutes later, they tow the plane out and it leaves."

"Anything else?"

"I talked to the guy who was working at the hanger that night and he doesn't remember anything. I've also checked with the Boca Police and the Florida Highway Patrol to see if they might have stopped anyone at the airport or on I 95 about the time the plane came in, but drew a blank there also," Bonner said.

"Are there any other cameras at the airport that we can check?"

"Already went around and asked. Negative."

"Alright then. Did you get a chance to talk with Goldman?" Robbie asked.

"Yeah and I found out that he has been going to the same restaurant for breakfast at the beginning of each shift. I talked with a waitress there and she said the same thing he did; he changed shifts because he was getting burned out at his other job."

"You ask him about the lack of phone calls?"

"He had a good answer. Said he didn't think the department would like him talking about an ongoing investigation. He also mentioned that he did talk to Cunningham about it, but that it was at Cunningham's house and not on the phone," Sam said.

Sam knew that this was not the news Robbie was hoping for, but he had to give him the facts. He also needed to report on what he saw when questioning Jay. Goldman had not been nervous and had been forthcoming with information. As far as he could tell, it was just a coincidence that Jay had changed shifts and was working when Maganelli was shot. He could also see that the waitress had some feelings for Jay, but he could not tell if Jay had felt the same way about her. Bonner knew that her feelings for Goldman could have clouded the information she had given him, but she seemed sincere when she said she was concerned about the pressures Jay had at his other job which led him to change his shift times. The bottom line was that he believed Goldman was telling the truth and that this was corroborated by a third party, even if this other person seemed to have feelings for Goldman.

Bonner sat and waited for a reaction from Robbie. He expected more questions or some sign that Robbie was getting irritated by the lack of progress in this case. Robbie however, sat silently looking at the files on his desk. Bonner began to stand up to leave when Robbie's phone rang. As Cappiello answered, he motioned for Sam to sit back down. It was Miller on the other end and Robbie put him on speaker so Bonner could hear what he had to say.

You could hear the frustration in Cappiello's voice as he asked Miller if he had found out anything which would help the case. Robbie had looked at his calendar when he was talking with Bonner and saw just how close he was to his retirement date. He wanted the arrest in this case, but to be more accurate, he needed this case. He couldn't put his finger on just why it was so important, but in his mind the results of this case would be his legacy within the department.

Miller didn't go through every detail; he just gave Cappiello the highlights. He had tried to find something that would have put all of the pieces together, but everything they had surmised during their initial investigation had been explained away. If McGuire and Barnes were in on the shooting, they had rehearsed their stories well. Besides, these were both experienced businessmen who worked in areas that were high risk. They each would have had years of experience in hiding their true feelings and motives during negotiations. Every question he had been sent out to get answered had a plausible explanation, even if the explanation did not fit what was considered normal. His gut told him differently, but he had nothing to prove that Cunningham's, McGuire's and Barnes' actions before, during and after the shooting were not just coincidental.

Robbie had listened without saying a word. When Miller finished, he told him to head on back to Plantation and to make sure everything he had learned was documented in the file. He was now wondering whether a "Cold Case" detective would retrieve this file sometime in the future and reopen the "unsolvable" case. Robbie's blood pressure went up as he gave thought to the fact that someone else might get the credit for something he and his team had put in countless hours trying to solve. If that was the case, he wanted to make sure that all of the information his team had collected would be in the file. This would not only help to solve the case in the future, but it would show the dedication and professionalism of each person who had worked on this investigation.

Robbie stood up after he hung up the phone and walked over to the white board on the wall. He looked at all the lines which connected the various people who had at one time or another had some involvement with his victim. He stood there silently wondering what connection he had missed. Which one of these intertwined groups had pulled this off? Cunningham was his shooter and he had gotten help from at least McGuire and LaBrock. McGuire appeared to be a dead end and LaBrock was out of jail on bond and there was no way Dietrich would allow any more questioning of his client by the police.

Bonner had sat silently through all of this and watched his boss as he studied the board. Sitting there, he realized that he was unsure of what exactly he was feeling at that moment. He could not decide if he felt sorry for Robbie because it now appeared that his last case would go unsolved or if he was actually pissed off because someone involved in this shooting turned out to be smarter than they were. Bonner knew there was nothing he could say that would change the way Robbie had to be feeling, so he stood up and asked if Cappiello needed him for anything else. Robbie just raised his hand in acknowledgement and Bonner knew this was his clue to leave Robbie to his own thoughts. He picked up his file from Robbie's desk and left the room.

Cappiello returned to his desk after a few minutes, sat down and began mindlessly leafing through one of the remaining files on his desk. In a few days there would be a retirement party in his honor. This would not only be attended by the officers and detectives he worked with, but by people in the community who he had become friends with over the years. There would be businessmen, defense attorneys and prosecutors there. The last two would put away their adversarial tendencies for the evening and even make jokes about cases or defendants they had been involved with. There would be the one nagging question which Robbie wished he had an answer for; whatever happened to that shooting case you were working on? He would have to smile and say that it was still under investigation, but that he was sure the new lead detective, Miller would have it wrapped up shortly. He sat alone in the detective bureau now wishing he didn't have to attend his own retirement party.

In the silence of the empty room, Robbie's thoughts turned to the "what if's". What if this case had occurred ten years before? Why could this not have happened in the summer of his career? He would have already developed the experience needed to deal with such a complicated case, but more importantly, he would have had the time he needed to see it through to its conclusion. Time was now something that he was in short supply of. He also came to the realization that if he was ten years younger, he most definitely would not have been as tired as he was now feeling. This case had taken a lot out of him, both physically and mentally. Maybe it was time to retire.

Robbie knew that he needed to stop worrying about things he had no control over. He took one last look at his white board and decided there was nothing more he could do on the case until morning. Miller would be back the next day, so he would get everyone together to go over everything one more time. He stood up and glanced at the white board as he left the room. He was hoping that he would recognize that one bit of overlooked information on the board which would tie everything together. Of course, he didn't see it and continued out the door.

CHAPTER 27

It was about an hour before visiting hours were over at the hospital. They had finally moved Vince out of intensive care. Bill had called ahead to make sure that Vince was allowed visitors and found out that he was in a private room. *Of course, Christine would have wanted Vince in his own room*, Bill thought to himself as he pulled into the hospital's parking lot. He stopped off in the gift shop to buy some flowers before heading up to room 415.

It took a minute for Bill's eyes to adjust to the low level of light in the room. The hallway of the hospital had been brightly lit, but Vince's room was very dark. There was one small light on above his bed which gave the room the appearance of twilight. Cunningham looked around and saw a figure sitting in a chair over in the corner of the room. This person stood up when Bill entered and he could just make out that it was a female. Bill continued into the room and the figure said, "May I help you." By now, the person had walked into what little light there was and Bill could see that it was a nurse. *Of course, a private nurse too.*

Bill heard the concern in the nurse's voice when she had first addressed him, so he knew he needed to reassure her. In a soft voice, which had just a touch of his southern accent thrown in, Bill said, "How are you tonight? I'm an old friend of Vince's and I just wanted to stop by and see how he was doing." Bill noted that the concern in the nurse's voice had instantly disappeared when she said, "Mr. Maganelli is still paralyzed if you were unaware of that. He can hear you and can answer yes and no questions by blinking his eyes. I can only give you a few minutes with him, so please make your visit brief."

"That's fine. I just wanted to leave these flowers and let him know I was thinking about him." The nurse must have been comfortable with Bill's explanation, because she excused herself and left the room. Bill placed the flowers on the serving table which was pushed up against the wall and grabbed the chair the nurse had been in. He slid it up next to Vince's bed and leaned over, so he could talk to Vince and not have his conversation over heard. It was then, after Bill's eyes had fully adjusted to the light in the room that he saw Vince's eyes. They showed the terror which Vince was now experiencing; he had to be wondering to himself why someone he had screwed over was now alone with him in the room. His eyes revealed the fact that Vince knew he would be unable to fight back and without the nurse in the room, he was totally at Bill's mercy. Bill of course, had the satisfaction of knowing he had created the precise atmosphere he wanted for his conversation with Vince.

"Calm down Vince. I'm not here to hurt you. I just wanted to talk a little," Bill said while still studying Vince's eyes, which were now frantically looking towards the door to see if the nurse was in sight.

"You know I struggled for months trying to figure out if I could kill you in cold blood. I've shot people before and never really had a problem with that, but you were different. I never knew any of them, but I do know you. On the other hand, none of them ever screwed me over like you did or caused me to lose my brother."

Bill continued to watch Vince's eyes. The terror never left his face as his eyes darted between looking at Bill and the hospital room door. Bill glanced over at Vince's heart monitor which was steadily rising. He knew they would be watching the monitor at the nurses' station, so he decided to make this quick.

"When it came down to it, I decided that I couldn't kill you, but turning you into a vegetable for the rest of your life was a different story. This way, it gives you ample time to look back on your miserable life, so you could realize what type of scumbag you really are. Do you have any idea how much time and practice went into making a shot that would have you end up this way instead of just killing you out right?"

Vince's heart monitor was now buzzing and it was time for Bill to leave.

"Just one more thing; I pulled the trigger, but Jim, Ken, Nicky and Jay all helped out and your buddy LaBrock, he's sitting in jail because they think he had something to do with it. It's all working out just the way we planned it. I hope you really enjoy the rest of your life."

It was about that time that two nurses came rushing in. Bill had moved to the foot of the bed and had a surprised look on his face. "I don't know what happened! I had just mentioned that I hoped we could get together when he gets out of here. You know, just giving him some hope when he started having problems," Bill said.

"Sir, we need you to leave," Vince's private nurse said.

"Sure! No problem, I'm sorry if I upset him," Bill said as he left the room. Cunningham stopped in the doorway and looked back to see one nurse checking the heart monitor and the other leaning over Vince. Vince's eyes were still fixed on him however, so Bill raised his right hand, shaped it into the form of a handgun and pointed it at Vince. Cunningham had hoped Vince didn't miss the smile on his face when he turned to finally leave the room.

Bill had missed something though. When the nurse had left the room after their first conversation, she smiled at him as she passed by. He thought that she was comfortable with his presence there when in fact; it was the unconscious smile of someone who was very nervous. She had immediately gone over to the nurse's station and picked up the phone. She pulled a business card from her pocket and dialed the phone number which was listed on the card. The nurse had a concerned look on her face as she continued to watch the open door to Vince's room while she waited for someone to pick up on the other end.

"This is Detective Cappiello."

"Detective, this is Jenny Myers, Mr. Maganelli's nurse. You told me to call if Mr. Maganelli had any visitors other than family."

"Yes, who's there?"

"I didn't get his name, but he said he was an old friend."

"Can you describe him please?" Jenny proceeded to give a very good description of Bill Cunningham; right down to his baby face. Robbie then told her to go back in the room to see if she couldn't confirm the visitor's identity which was about the same time the alarm on Vince's heart monitor sounded. She laid the phone down without saying anything else. Robbie waited a few minutes, but decided that Jenny must have gotten distracted with one of her patients. He decided that he had better head over to the hospital to see for himself what was going on.

After Bill Cunningham left Vince's room, he went to his car and sat for a few minutes in the hospital's parking lot. He started mentally going over everything which had transpired up to that point. He was actually pleased with himself that he had not killed Vince, even though that had been his initial intent. He did realize that he was a little more sadistic than he would have liked to think he was, but this was an unusual circumstance. He wanted Vince to suffer the way he had. Bill would never have a brother to talk to again and it was fitting that Vince wouldn't be talking to anyone either.

It was now going to be the right time to tell Laura what he had done and what the outcome of his actions were going to mean to her. Bill was confident that he knew how Laura would react to the news. Laura hated Vince as much as he did. He just hoped that she wouldn't think any less of him for doing what, in his mind and the minds of Dave's friends needed to be done. Bill knew how much Laura had missed Dave. He had not only been her brother-in-law, he was her friend. She had been able to talk to Dave about Bill and he had given her insight into her husband's personality which she would have never learned on her own. Bill was loving, but not the most open person on the planet or the easiest to talk to.

Bill drove home from the hospital and stopped along the way to pick up a bottle of wine. *"I'll need all the help I can get,"* Bill thought to himself as he waited to pay for the wine. When he finally arrived home, he found Laura in the den working at her desk. He was getting cold feet about talking to her, but forced himself to go in and took a seat next to hers.

"I've got something I want to talk to you about and it's very important," he said. Laura looked at Bill and saw in his face that whatever it was, he was very concerned about it. She closed her computer and turned to face him.

"Ok, you have my attention," she said.

"I've never kept anything from you before and I should have told you about this from the beginning, but I didn't. Do you remember when the detectives talked to me and you asked if I had anything to do with Vince getting shot?"

Laura stared into Bill's face for a minute. She still saw the same face she had fallen in love with fifteen years earlier. He had always provided and cared for her, not because he had to, but because he loved her and she knew that. She also knew that he would never do anything to hurt her. She finally spoke up.

"Thank God. I thought you were going to tell me you had a girlfriend."

"This is serious," Bill said.

"Yes dear, I know it is. I've known you had something to do with Vince getting shot ever since you gave that detective that asinine smile you always give me when you're hiding something."

"I need to tell you what's going on."

"No, you don't. I don't really want to know what your part was. I hated him as much as you did, if not more. He took away our future, he took away your brother and my friend and he ruined our friends' lives. As far as I'm concerned, he deserved it and I don't want to discuss it anymore."

"Well there is one part of all of this that you will have to know about. It's going to involve our future together."

"Bill, as long as you and I are together, I don't care where it is or under what conditions. You just need to know I'm there for you and we'll get through this just like every other time we've had a problem."

"Ok, but trust me. We are not going to have any problems in the future."

"I do trust you." She leaned over and kissed him on the cheek saying, "I wouldn't care if we had to live on a beach somewhere."

"Funny you should say that. That's exactly what I had in mind. You see, I had a partner in all of this and we have some money waiting for us in a bank in the Cayman Islands."

"Money? How much? You didn't steal it, did you?"

"No I didn't steal it. It was part of the deal to get Vince out of the picture. We have just a little over two million."

"Did you say million?" Laura said as she almost fell out of her chair. The look on her face was one of total disbelief and shock. She sat in her chair for a minute or so staring at Bill. She was in shock; she just kept going over and over in her head what her husband had just said. "You did say million?" she asked one more time.

"Like I said, I had a partner in this and we sat down and figured out what Cunningham would have been worth. That's where the figure came from. My partner had it transferred to the Cayman Islands after Vince was shot. It's just sitting there waiting for us to show up and claim it."

"You keep saying "your partner". Who is it?"

"This thing is not over yet. Its best you don't know. If for some reason Detective Cappiello is smarter than I give him credit for, it would be better if you didn't know the names of those involved. If something happens, you need to get on the first plane you can and go down to the Caymans."

"I would never leave you behind."

"Like I said, you need to trust me. I have a contact that will get me out of that too. I've worked on this plan for two years. Why did you think I went to Iraq for a year; for the scenery?"

"Ok. I'll do what you want, but don't get yourself arrested. I can't spend that much money by myself."

Bill didn't answer and leaned over to give his wife a kiss. He wasn't going to get himself arrested. He had an exit plan already in place. Bill had one more bit of information to share with his wife that he was sure she was going to like. He was not going to make it easy for Detective Cappiello. Bill had decided that now was a good time to make himself unavailable to the detective and any further questioning. If Cappiello wanted to talk to him; he was going to need a plane ticket.

"We're going on a little trip," Bill said.

"When and where." Laura said with a somewhat cautious tone to her voice.

"Tomorrow and you'll need to pack for a long trip."

"Right!" Laura said, tilting her head and rolling her eyes as she spoke.

"I'm serious. I have us booked on a flight to the Caymans tomorrow morning and we'll be gone a month or so. I've already packed up some of our stuff and we're going to drop it off at Nicky's on the way to the airport."

"You're serious!"

"Yes, I am. Pack the things you want to keep and don't worry about the rest. We're not coming back here for awhile."

She knew Bill was serious by the look he had when he spoke to her. Laura glanced around the room and could not decide where to begin. They had few possessions which meant much to either of them, except for a few family photos and items which had belonged to their parents. She was sure that everything she would want to keep would fit into a couple of boxes.

"What are we going to do about the house?" Laura asked.

"I contacted a real estate agent who is going to list the house. The sign will be up first thing tomorrow morning."

"I guess with two million we can get another house." she said.

"I would hope so. I gave the agent the name of an attorney if she needs to get in touch with us. I also told her that Nicky had permission to go into the house just in case you remember something you forgot and can't live without."

"I guess I had better get to packing then. Where are our passports?"

Bill smiled and left the room, leaving Laura behind. She sat quietly for a few minutes trying to imagine what it would be like to have that much money. She came to the conclusion that she couldn't and left it at that.

It was about forty five minutes after Cunningham had left the hospital when Detective Cappiello stopped by the nurse's station outside of Vince's room to talk to Jenny Myers. He had a picture of Cunningham with him and she confirmed that he was the person who had visited Maganelli. She did not overhear what was said, but he had only been in the room a few minutes before Maganelli's heart monitor's alarm sounded. Cappiello looked at his watch and even though he was anxious to confront Cunningham about his visit, he decided that it would have to wait until morning. Miller had just gotten back from his trip and Bonner had put in several long days. Both were undoubtedly tired and would want to sleep. He was tired too. Once again, it had been a long day.

CHAPTER 28

Cappiello had lost a lot of sleep that night thinking about Cunningham's visit to the hospital. This could be the one little item that could start to unravel Cunningham's story, if not his confidence. It sometimes turns out that it's the seemingly insignificant events, which might be overlooked by others that end up solving cases. Robbie, if he formulated his questions properly just might be able to trip up Cunningham or get him to say something he wished he hadn't. He was going to give it one more try.

Robbie decided that the morning meeting could wait. This was more important. As soon as Miller showed up at the station, the two of them drove over to Cunningham's house. As the house came into sight, Cappiello couldn't believe what he was seeing. "Holy shit," he said out loud as he pulled into the driveway. "What the hell," was Miller's response when he finally saw the sign that was now sitting in the front yard of the Cunningham home. The words "For Sale", which were printed in bold red letters on the sign was what they had both responded to.

Miller was getting out of the vehicle before it even came to a stop and went up to the front door. Meanwhile, Robbie was busy dialing the number for the sales agent who was listed on the sign. Miller walked back to the car and found that Robbie was on hold.

"The house is still furnished, but all the pictures and things that were on the walls are gone."

Robbie held up a finger to interrupt Miller as the agent came on the phone.

"This is Cathy, my I help you?"

"Yes Cathy. This is Detective Cappiello of the Plantation Police Department. I need some information about a listing you have on Camellia Court."

"Yes, the Cunningham home. Just got that listing yesterday. It's a beautiful four bedroom, three baths with a pool. It's got…" Robbie stopped her sales pitch right there.

"Cathy, I'm not interested in the house. We're conducting a criminal investigation and I need to talk to the owner."

"That won't be possible. The Cunningham's went out of town this morning." Robbie covered his forehead with his large, beefy hand and rubbed it up and down on his face. He had just developed a huge head ache.

"Did they leave a forwarding address or a way to get in touch with them?"

"No. I'm to get in touch with them through their lawyer," Cathy said.

Robbie thanked her for the information and hung up. He then threw his cell phone as hard as he could at the side of his police car. "I don't believe this shit. I had him and he got away," Robbie yelled as he turned and leaned back against his car in disgust. He stood there for a few minutes, just staring at the ground. Miller stood nearby, looking at the house and knew there was nothing he could say to Robbie.

About the time this was happening, Bill and Laura were sitting down in the Delta departure lounge in the Ft. Lauderdale International Airport. They were involved in some small talk when Laura's attention was drawn to a lady who was walking towards them.

"What is she doing here?" Laura asked Bill as Christine Maganelli walked up and stood in front of them.

"I told you I had a partner," Bill said.

Bill stood up and gave Christine a kiss on the cheek. "Let's go over there where we can talk," Bill said to his two female companions as he pointed to an unoccupied corner of the departure lounge.

Laura was not sure how to take this. Bill had despised Vince and now he had his wife for a partner? Laura sat down in a chair across from Bill and Christine with her arms crossed and an "I'm not pleased" look on her face waiting for an explanation.

"I know this doesn't look good, but Bill was the only one I could turn to who I knew I could trust. Vince has been verbally and physically abusive towards me for years. I took it as long as I could. The last straw was when I saw what he did to you guys and Jim. I really liked the three of you and couldn't stand what he did to you. I decided that he needed to be stopped. He wouldn't give me a divorce, so I asked Bill for some help."

"Bill said there was money waiting for us. Did it come from you," Laura asked.

"I wanted to make sure that I would be taken care of, no matter how this turned out. I also wanted you to have what was due to you, so I made sure the money was transferred. It was Jim's idea. I use to sign papers at home which Vince couldn't be bothered to sign. I became really good at his signature, so all I did was type up the request, sign it and give it to LaBrock. He's a shady shit and thought Vince was pulling a fast one on the IRS, so he was more than willing to go along."

"Is LaBrock involved? Why did he get arrested?" Laura said.

"We wanted the police to concentrate on someone other than us. Besides, he's a slime ball and deserves anything he gets. We set up a phony business offer and LaBrock fell for it. He made all of the arrangements only he didn't know he was talking to some actor Jim had found to play the part of an investor. Nicky made the final call which got Vince out of the house on a disposable cell phone. He gave it to me later and I wiped the prints off of it. I met Christine one day at her gym and gave her the phone," Bill said.

Christine then spoke up. "I took the phone to LaBrock's office the day I gave him the transfer authorization from Vince. I asked him to make a copy for me and when he left the office, I put it in his credenza. Bill knew that between John's background, the meeting with the investor which the police would find out was phony and the money transfers, they would be searching John's office."

"Nicky was involved? Who else," Laura asked.

"The whole group; Jim, Ken, Nicky and even Jay. They don't know it yet, but they are all getting a share of the money Christine had transferred. Jim is getting the same as you and I and the other three are going to split about two million," Bill said.

Bill also could not resist telling Laura how he played with the detective's minds a little.

"Do you remember sitting in the bar the day the news reported that they were going to make some arrests very soon?" Bill asked Laura. "I was the one who made the call to Channel 4 just to piss off that detective; Cappiello. I knew he would get side tracked and try to find out who leaked the information to the press."

Laura was not sure if she should be pissed or admire his moxie. All three sat for a couple of minutes thinking about what had just been discussed when Christine spoke up.

"I stopped by the hospital on the way here, just so Vince would know I had a part in this too. I also wanted him to know that I was leaving him and he didn't need to ask for a divorce, even if he could. I was finally going to enjoy myself and still have all the advantages that his money would supply. After the three of us stop by the bank in the Caymans, I'm heading off to Paris."

Laura sat quietly for a few more minutes. She had wanted to ask if Bill had pulled the trigger, but she had told him once that she didn't want to know about his involvement and that is what she was going to stick to. She wanted to keep the image of him that she had fallen in love with. Everything he had ever done was for her and she guessed that was part of the reason he had agreed to do this. She would have never guessed that Christine would have set this up. She just didn't seem to be the type. Laura also never knew that Vince was abusive, but that part really didn't surprise her. He was such an ass. She was happy about one thing though; Vince was still alive. In her mind, no one deserved it more to be dead, but this way, he would be forced to live with his actions for the rest of his life. If, in fact Bill was the shooter, she was actually glad that he hadn't killed him in cold blood.

Her thought process was suddenly interrupted by the gate's public address announcer,

"Delta flight 1527 to Grand Cayman is ready for boarding at gate…"

www.ingramcontent.com/pod-product-compliance
Lightning Source LLC
Chambersburg PA
CBHW060448300726

48975CB00008B/2434